With a little sob, she was in his arms.

Gage kissed her mouth, her eyes, her temples. He felt like a drowning man clutching a bit of driftwood. If he held on too loosely, she might slip from his grasp; too tightly, and he might overwhelm her.

Natalie solved the problem for him. She moaned, lifted herself to him, dug her hands into his hair and crushed his mouth to hers.

"Baby." His voice caught and broke; he clasped her face in his hands and kissed her, deep and hard. "Oh, my sweet baby."

Her hands swept under his jacket. She felt the race of his heart, knew it matched the galloping beat of her own.

"Yes," she said, "oh, yes, please. Please...."

THE BARONS

Four brothers—
bonded by inheritance, battling for love!

Jonas Baron is approaching his eighty-fifth
birthday. He has ruled Espada, his sprawling
estate in Texas hill country, for more than
forty years, but now he admits it's time he
chose an heir.

Jonas has three sons, Gage, Travis and Slade, all
ruggedly good-looking and each with a successful
business empire of his own; none wishes to give
up the life he's fought for to take over Espada.
Jonas also has a stepdaughter; beautiful and
spirited, Caitlin loves the land as much as he
does, but she's not of the Baron blood.

So who will receive Baron's bequest? As Gage,
Travis, Slade and Caitlin discover, there's more at
stake than Espada. For love also has its part to
play in deciding their futures....

Sit back now and enjoy Gage's story, and be sure
to look out next for **More Than a Mistress** in
August (Harlequin Presents #2045), when you'll
get to know Travis a whole lot better!

SANDRA MARTON

Marriage on the Edge

THE BARONS

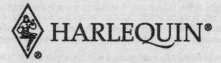

HARLEQUIN®

TORONTO • NEW YORK • LONDON
AMSTERDAM • PARIS • SYDNEY • HAMBURG
STOCKHOLM • ATHENS • TOKYO • MILAN • MADRID
PRAGUE • WARSAW • BUDAPEST • AUCKLAND

ISBN 0-373-12027-3

MARRIAGE ON THE EDGE

First North American Publication 1999.

CHAPTER ONE

GAGE BARON was not in the best of moods.

He'd put in a long day, riding herd on a contractor and construction crew that seemed to have forgotten the idea was to build a new wing onto Baron's Windsong Resort, not to demolish it.

Now he was about to put in an even tougher night, though given a choice, Gage thought wryly, he'd trade the company of the elite gathering at the Holcombs's cocktail party for the earthy reality of the construction bunch anytime.

But he had given his word he'd attend, which meant he had to go to the silly thing, like it or not.

"Damn fool thing to have done, Baron," he muttered to his reflection in the bathroom mirror. "But you did it, and you're stuck with it."

Gage scraped the sharp edge of his razor across his jaw. Bad enough a man had to shave every morning but to have to do it all over again at six in the evening seemed unconscionable.

He glanced at the gold Rolex that lay on the edge of the sink. Not six. Seven-fifteen. He was late, on top of everything else...although, now that he thought about it, being late wasn't so bad. There'd be one less hour of standing around the Holcomb patio, pretending he was having a good time when only an idiot would have a good time at a stupid cocktail party for Liz Holcomb's latest pet charity.

And who did he have to blame? Gage scowled at his reflection as he rinsed the lather from his face. Himself, that was who. Himself, and nobody else.

He'd let Natalie talk him into it. "I'll skip the party and send a check," he'd said, when she'd shown him the invitation. "You just tell me how big the check should be." But

5

Natalie had given him that look, the one he'd seen on her lovely face more and more the past few months.

"You're free to do that, if you wish," she'd said in that cool and elegant voice of hers, "but I worked on the committee with Liz."

"Meaning?" Gage had countered, and Natalie had smiled politely and said meaning, of course, that she'd be attending the cocktail party even if he didn't.

Her reply had surprised him. Things had gotten off track between them lately but still, they were a couple. Weren't they? For one long moment, he'd almost asked her that but he'd thought better of it and said, okay, if it meant so much to her, he'd go.

"Thank you," Natalie had said, her tone as polite as her smile, and that had thrown him off balance again, made him so damned furious he'd wanted to haul her into his arms, kiss her until she turned back into the woman he remembered.

The breath hissed from between Gage's teeth. He tossed aside the towel, strapped on his watch and strode, naked, into his bedroom.

But sex was supposed to be a two-way street. And in life, just as in business, you never went into a situation unless you were pretty damn sure you knew the outcome...and who knew what would have happened if he'd tried to melt Natalie's icy politeness with sex?

It might not have worked. And that was a possibility he wasn't ready to face just yet.

On the other hand, he'd figured that maybe it was time to push for some answers. Gage paused at the door to his closet, his jaw tightening. Maybe it was time to find out if it was only his ego that wanted Natalie warm and responsive in his arms, and not his heart.

So he'd told her that he'd be delighted to go to the Holcomb party, now that he knew she'd had a hand in the planning, and he'd even thought her polite smile had warmed a little.

"Thank you," she'd said, and he'd started making plans right then and there to be at his charming best the night of the party and see if he couldn't recapture some of what used to be between Natalie and him.

Now, those plans had gone up in smoke because he was waltzing off to the Holcombs all by himself.

"Big surprise, Baron," he muttered as he slid open the closet door.

It seemed as if he couldn't count on anything much lately. Plans, except the ones that involved iron-clad contracts and rock-hard commitments, were meaningless. People were unpredictable; feelings came and went in the blink of an eye, and if he'd been fool enough to think Natalie would be any different, he was starting to learn otherwise.

Gage's mouth thinned.

If it was over with Natalie, it was over. And maybe it was for the best. What was the point in a relationship in which silence had replaced conversation and accommodation had replaced passion?

"Is there something wrong?" he'd said a couple of weeks ago. God, what the words had cost him, especially when he'd seen the look of disdain that had crept over Natalie's beautiful face.

"I don't know," she'd said in that polite voice that made his blood pressure zoom. "You tell me. Is there?"

For the first time in his life, Gage had considered that it was possible, just possible, that a man might have a reason for slugging a woman. Well, if the woman were a man. If she were as big as he was, at six feet two, or if her muscles had been hardened by years of physical labor before things started coming together right.

But Natalie was none of those things. She was tall, yes, and with a toned, beautiful body, but she was definitely all woman.

He would never hurt her. Never. And yet, it didn't seem to mean a damn to her that she was hurting him. Okay, not hurting him. How could she, when he didn't really feel the same way about her anymore? Still, he was entitled to common courtesy. And after ten years of marriage, it looked as if Natalie had even given up on that.

"She knew I was only going to this damned party because of her," Gage said to the open closet. "But did she phone my office to say she wouldn't be going with me? No," he growled, answering his own question. "No, she did not."

No call. No explanation. Nothing but the red light blinking on the answering machine to greet him as he came in the door half an hour ago, and then Natalie's clipped voice saying, "I've been delayed. I'm not promising anything but if I possibly can, I'll meet you at the Holcombs's."

At least she'd gotten that right, he thought grimly, as he shouldered his way into a white dress shirt. No promises. And now, no Natalie.

"So, here you are, Baron, going to this party alone," Gage muttered as he zipped up his fly, then slipped on his jacket. "What do you think that makes you, huh?"

A jerk, that was what. A jerk in a tuxedo. He glared into the mirror, ran his hands through his dark hair, adjusted his bow tie, tried a smile and wondered if people would run in terror when he tried it on them.

This was going to be one terrific night. He'd shelled out a thousand bucks to spend the evening trapped in a monkey suit, munching soggy canapés, drinking flat champagne, wondering where Natalie was...

And why the hell *should* he? Gage's pale blue eyes narrowed. Natalie was a big girl. She could take care of herself, as she was so fond of telling him.

If it was over, it was over. The sooner he got used to the idea, the better.

Gage plucked his car keys from the top of his dresser, tossed them in the air, and headed for the door.

The lineup of cars headed for the Holcomb mansion began half a block from the driveway.

"Great," Gage muttered, as he eased down through the gears of his vintage Corvette, "just great."

There was nothing like being stuck on the tail end of a line of Caddies and Mercedes to make a man wish he were sitting in the lounge of the Baron Windsong, enjoying a glass of vintage *chinon blanc.*

The Cadillac ahead of him jerked forward a couple of inches. Gage sighed as he moved the Vette up behind it.

Never mind the wine. Never mind the hotel. He saw enough of it during the day, and wine was a great idea, given the right time and place, but just now what would really do it was a chilled bottle of a good dark ale. And a beach, not here in Miami but somewhere out in the South Pacific, where that same big, white moon that was floating overhead would cast its ivory light over an untouched stretch of sand. Man, he could just see it. He'd be in a pair of cut-down denims, leaning back on his elbows, his face turned up to the night sky as he watched all those falling stars flame through the blackness while the cool surf kissed his toes...

A horn beeped behind him. Gage blinked, frowned, saw the car-length space that had opened before him, and eased the Vette forward.

What was wrong with him tonight?

It was years since he'd sat on a beach, or wanted to; years since he'd spent so much time in foolish introspection...

Years since a woman had made him feel so uncertain.

His hands flexed on the steering wheel.

This couldn't go on. Okay, he'd endure the Holcomb shindig for an hour. Half an hour; that would be enough. Then he'd slip out the door, confront Natalie when she finally showed up at home, demand answers, and end the nonsense between them one way or the other.

If she wanted to go on, he'd consider it. If she wanted to finish things, so be it. Life would go on, divorce or not...

In which case, what was he doing here, waiting his turn to go to a party he didn't want to attend, courtesy of a woman he wasn't sure he wanted anymore?

That was the truth, and admitting it, finally, made him feel as if a weight had been lifted from his chest.

To hell with this. Gage's jaw tightened. He'd cut out of line, go back to the house, peel off this silly suit, climb into his cutoffs...

"Sir?"

He could feel the knot in his gut start to loosen. All he had to do was back up a couple of inches, thread the Vette's nose out into the road...

"Sir? Excuse me, sir?"

Gage jerked his head towards the window. "What?" he snarled, and blinked.

Without realizing it, he'd reached the driveway. A kid stood outside the car, his red jacket pronouncing him the parking attendant for the night. His face was pimply, his Adam's apple was bobbing, and Gage sighed, tamped down his temper, and once again managed that thing he hoped might pass for a smile.

"Yeah," he said, and because fate had intervened, or he'd taken too damn long to come to his senses, he did what any man would do under the circumstances, stepped out of the Vette, handed the kid his keys along with a ten dollar bill to make up for the way he'd snarled, and climbed the steps of the Holcomb mansion to what he knew would be a couple of hours of brutally civilized torture.

Torture was too polite a word.

Who was it who'd invented cocktail parties, anyway? Charity ones, especially? Not a man, he was certain of that. Only a woman would expect human beings to pay for the privilege of standing in a crowded room clutching a glass of undrinkable wine in one hand and a lump of inedible something in the other, while a string quartet on the patio sawed its way through something that had probably been just as dull and lifeless when it was written a couple of hundred years ago as it was now.

The smile he'd practiced seemed to be working well enough. It made him feel like an escapee from a funny farm but nobody seemed put off by it. Hank Holcomb had pumped his hand, muttered something about how pleased he was to be hosting the party even as he rolled his eyes in denial. Liz Holcomb had swooped down in a cloud of perfume dense enough to gas anybody around her, air-kissed both his cheeks and urged him to try the battered shrimp.

"Where's our Natalie?" Liz had said, but she'd squealed at the sight of someone else before he'd had to come up with an answer. "I'll see you later, darling," she'd cried, kissed the air in his general direction, and flown off.

So he'd wandered through the football-field-size living room, out to the patio, back through the dining room, accepted the glass of wine and the limp canapé from passing waiters once he grew weary of saying, "No, thanks," every two minutes, and now he'd found himself a fairly quiet spot in a corner nobody coveted because the potted palm that filled it did an effective job of shielding from view whoever might stand beneath its overhanging fronds and, after all, he supposed, half the purpose of attending this thing was the dubious pleasure of seeing and being seen.

And the longer he stood there, observing the scene, the better he felt. There was something about the silliness of it all. The bad food. The worse wine. The awful music. The guests, the women, glittering like brightly plumaged birds; the men, decked out like penguins. He chuckled. It was like being inside some enormous aviary. Even the sounds in the room seemed appropriate. Cluck, cluck. Cheep, cheep…

"Hi."

He turned. The voice was soft and sultry; it went magnificently with the face and body, which were, without question, the best good genes and plastic surgery had to offer.

"Hi," he said, and smiled.

"Awful, isn't it?" the woman said.

Gage laughed. "Absolutely."

"The wine. The hors d'oeuvres." She shuddered in a way he figured she'd spent lots of time perfecting. It made her long, straight mane of golden hair slip over her bare shoulders like water running over alabaster and her rounded breasts quiver like Jell-O beneath the couple of inches of fabric that was supposed to be a dress. She tilted her head, looked up at him through her lashes and, very slowly, trailed the tip of her tongue across her moist bottom lip. "Why," she said, with a lazy smile, "I just don't know what to do with myself."

A muscle danced in Gage's jaw. He'd been out of circulation for a while but a man would have to be dead from the neck up and the waist down not to know what the answer to that remark was supposed to be.

I do, he was supposed to say, and the gorgeous blonde with the impossible boobs would smile again, link her arm through his, and not too long after, they'd be in bed.

His body tightened reflexively at the sudden image. It was a long time since he'd thought about having a woman other than Natalie. Too long, maybe. Maybe that was just what he needed, a hot broad, a mindless tussle between cool sheets, a mutual wham-bam-thank-you-ma'am, with no morning-after regrets, no recriminations, no commitments that would only screw up his head.

"Yes or no?" the blonde said softly, her baby blues filled with a directness Gage could admire if not accept.

He smiled, a little regretfully.

"Sorry. I'm just not..."

"That's all right." Her smile was regretful, too. "Another time, perhaps."

"Sure," he said, although he knew he didn't mean it. Even if things ended with Natalie, even after he was free to move on, he'd be done with women. For a while, anyway, he thought, as the blonde sauntered away. A man would have to be either a fool or a liar to swear off the female of the species completely but right now, for the foreseeable future, he had no wish whatsoever to—to—

That was when he saw her, in the doorway.

His breath caught, his stomach tightened, and he knew his thoughts of a moment ago had been all lies.

He wasn't done with women, not for tonight, not for the foreseeable future, not any way, any shape, any time.

The woman in the doorway was the most beautiful creature he'd ever seen.

It was wrong to compare her to the blonde who'd just

moved off but the contrasts were so incredible that he couldn't keep from doing it.

She wasn't blonde. Maybe that didn't seem like much but in Miami Beach, in this kind of crowd, most of the heads were golden. Not that they'd started life that way. It was just that the sun seemed to inspire a sun-kissed look.

Not for her.

The lady coming slowly down the steps into the living room had hair as black as night. She wore it drawn back from her perfect oval face, knotted high on her head; just looking at it, Gage could tell that when she let it down—when *he* let it down, it would flow over his hands like ebony silk.

His gaze wandered over her, taking in the wide, dark eyes, the straight nose, the determined mouth, dropped lower to skim over her simple black dress, over what he knew had to be breasts that had not been fashioned by the surgeon's knife. She was slender, this woman, but she was all woman nonetheless, with sweetly curved hips and long, gorgeous legs encased in sheer black hose that ended in black sandals with impossibly high heels.

She was beautiful, more beautiful than any woman he'd ever seen, and she was alone. Alone, but searching the room for someone.

Gage ditched the silly canapé and sorry excuse for a drink in the potted palm. If she was looking for a man, that man was damned well going to be him.

He stepped out from the corner, his eyes fastened to her, and waited. She would look towards him; every instinct, every thump of his heart told him so.

And, at last, she did.

Their eyes met and held. Time seemed to stop; the moment stretched out between them, filled with heat. Gage could feel his blood thickening as it pumped through his veins. His body had reacted to the blonde, but not like this.

This was different. It was everything he'd ever hoped for, or dreamed.

Something flickered across her lovely face. Eagerness? Anticipation? He took a step forward...and saw something else on her face. Panic. Even fear. Hell, why would she fear him? She knew what he wanted; it was what she wanted, too, he was sure of it.

He took another step and she whirled away from him, vanishing into the crowd.

She was running from him but, dammit, he wasn't going to let her get away. Not tonight. Not when she was what he needed, what he'd hungered for without even knowing he was hungry.

He moved quickly, knifing his way through the clots of people filling the room, his gaze constant in its search for a flash of that pale face, that silken hair.

Liz Holcomb grasped his arm.

"Gage, you gorgeous man, there you are! I want you to meet…"

"Later," he said, and swept past her.

Hank was next, appearing suddenly in his path with a portly, smiling gentleman in tow.

"Gage, old pal, here's the mayor of…"

"Later," he said again, and kept moving…and, all at once, he saw her, hurrying out the French doors to the patio.

She was almost running, wobbling slightly in those ridiculously high heels, those sexy-as-sin heels. Past the string quartet, down the garden steps, past the fountain where cherubs and dolphins cavorted in cascades of illuminated water. Just beyond the fountain she paused, looked back. Their eyes met again and the heat he saw in hers almost made him groan.

Still, she turned and fled. Gage quickened his pace. There was no need to run. He was faster than she was and he knew she couldn't escape him, not out here. The garden was walled; there was no way out.

He knew, too, that she didn't really want to escape him.

It had been there, in her eyes. The need. The urgency. The hot wanting that pulsed through her body just as it pulsed through his.

And there she was, at last. She stood in the rear of the garden, where the darkness had gathered, where the leafy branches of the trees blocked out all but the faintest hint of moonlight.

Gage stopped, inches from her.

Her eyes were wide, her lips were parted. She was breathing hard, and her breasts rose and fell quickly beneath the clinging black dress. A strand of hair had slipped free of the pins that held it and trailed down her neck. Her scent, an erotic blend of jasmine and roses mixed with the scent of the sea beyond the garden wall, filled his senses.

He reached out. She drew back.

"Are you afraid of me?" he said softly.

She licked her lips. Nothing in the way she did it was provocative, yet the simple gesture made his body harden like stone.

He came closer, so close that he knew he had only to bend his head if he wanted to brush her mouth with his.

"I won't hurt you," he murmured. "Surely you know that."

"You won't mean to," she said. Her voice was low and husky. The sound of it seemed to dance against his skin. "But you will."

"No." He said the word fiercely but the hand he reached out was gentle as he tucked the trailing strands of hair behind her ear. "No," he said again, "I'd never hurt you."

"You will," she whispered, "you—"

And then, with a little sob, she was in his arms.

Gage kissed her mouth, her eyes, her temples. He knew he was holding her too closely, that he might be bruising her delicate bones, but he felt like a drowning man clutching a bit of driftwood. If he held on too loosely, she might slip from his grasp; too tightly, and he might overwhelm her.

She solved the problem for him. She moaned, lifted herself to him, dug her hands into his hair and crushed his mouth to hers.

"Babe." His voice caught and broke; he clasped her face in his hands and kissed her, deep and hard. "Oh, my sweet babe."

Her hands swept under his jacket, her palms spreading

across his chest. She felt the race of his heart, knew it matched the galloping beat of her own.

"Yes," she said, "oh, yes, please. Please..."

She groaned when he dragged down the straps of her dress. The swell of her breasts above the lacy filigree of her bra shone like fresh cream in the moonlight. She cried out when he buried his face in her neck. Her head fell back; he cupped her breasts, bit lightly at her skin, slipped his hands beneath the bra and touched the eager flesh that awaited him.

Her answering cry tore away whatever thin veneer of civilized behavior that remained to him. He made a sound deep in his throat, drew her further into the darkness, pressed her back against the wall.

She whispered something he couldn't understand as he thrust his hands up under her skirt. Her hips tilted towards his; he brushed his palm over the scrap of lace that covered her. She was hot, wet enough so he could feel the slickness of her through the lace; she burned like molten lava against his questing fingertips.

He groaned, and ripped the lace away. "Come to me," he whispered...

"No!"

Her cry rose into the night, sharp and piercing as the gust of wind that had suddenly come from the sea. Gage didn't hear it. He was lost, blind to everything but the feel of her in his arms, the taste of her on his lips. It had been so long. So long...

"No." Her hand clamped over his; she twisted her face away from his seeking mouth. "Stop it," she panted, "Damn you, I said stop!"

The urgency in her voice, the combined anger and fear, snapped him back to reality. He went still, his body numb as he became aware of her struggles. He blinked his eyes, like a man who has gazed too long at the sun, and looked down into her face.

"What?" he said. "What?"

She was trembling and she hated herself for that, hated herself almost as much as she did for having succumbed, for having let herself be caught up in one blind, foolish moment of passion.

"Let go of me," she whispered.

Let go of her? Let go of her, when she'd just been coming apart like a falling star in his arms?

"Let go," she said again, and what he heard in her voice now vanquished whatever dream had held him. Reality was her cold voice, her cold eyes...

Her contempt.

The fire inside him died. He stepped back, adjusted his tie, smoothed down his shirt. She fixed her shoulder straps, tugged down her skirt.

"That's a dangerous game you were playing, lady," he said, when he could trust himself to speak.

Her eyes flashed. "You were the one playing games, not me."

"Dancing a man to the edge and then telling him to behave himself might win you applause in some quarters, babe, but sooner or later, you're liable to do that to a man who doesn't give a damn about the rules."

She wrapped her arms around herself. It was hot out here in the garden, but the wind carried a chill in its teeth, or maybe the chill was inside her; it was impossible to tell and she didn't much care. All that mattered was how close, how dangerously close, she'd come to falling into the trap again.

"I suppose you think I was the one who stalked you."

"Stalked?"

She heard the growl in his voice, knew he was angry, but so what? She was angry, too, dammit, angry and hurt.

"Stalked," she said. "Followed me, even though I made it perfectly clear I was trying to get away from you."

Gage gave a bark of laughter. "Give me a break! You wanted me to come after you. I saw the way you looked at me. I understood what it meant."

"It's just a good thing you finally figured out what 'no' meant. Otherwise—"

"Otherwise, what?" A slow smile crept across his mouth. He reached out, traced a finger over her parted lips. "Be honest, baby. If I'd ignored that 'no,' I'd be inside you right now and you'd be—"

The crack of her hand against his cheek echoed through the silence of the night.

"You no good bastard!"

Her voice trembled. She despised herself for it, for the weakness that had sent her into his arms...and for the knowledge that he was right. For all those reasons and a thousand more, Natalie Baron lifted her chin, met her husband's angry glare and spoke the words she'd once never imagined herself saying, the words she'd bitten back over the last endless months.

"Gage," she said, "I want a divorce."

CHAPTER TWO

THE sound of a lawnmower woke Natalie from a fitful sleep.

She blinked her eyes open, then shut them against the bright sunlight that poured into the room. That was a surprise. Hadn't Gage remembered to close the blinds before he'd come to bed? It was something he always did, for her. The light didn't bother him but she...

"Oh, God."

Natalie's whisper rose into the still morning air. Of course Gage hadn't closed the blinds. This wasn't their bedroom, this was the guest room. She and Gage hadn't shared a bed last night.

Her throat constricted.

For the first time since the night they'd eloped, she and her husband had slept apart.

Well, no. Not exactly. Slowly, she sat up and swung her feet to the carpeted floor. Actually, they'd slept apart lots of times. More and more times, in fact, over the past year and a half. Gage was always off on business trips, exploring new sites for Baron Resorts, talking high finance with bankers from Bangkok to Baltimore, checking out the competition...

Or so he said.

Natalie pushed a fall of dark hair back from her face. She rose and made her way into the attached bathroom, trying to avoid seeing her reflection, but it wasn't easy. The interior designer who'd "done" the bath had covered the walls with mirrors. Since the room was the size of the first apartment she and Gage had lived in, that meant lots of mirrors. Acres, or so it sometimes seemed. It wasn't what she would have done—what woman in her right mind really wanted her reflection beaming back at her from every angle, first thing in the morning? But Gage had given the designer carte blanche.

"Everything subject to my wife's approval, of course,"

he'd said, standing there with his arm around Natalie's shoulder.

"Of course, Mr. Baron," the designer had replied, casting a fawning smile in her direction.

"Just don't bother her with details," Gage had added, with a just-between-us-guys grin. "My wife has enough to do without worrying about chips of paint." He'd beamed down at her. "The country club tennis tournament, her charities...isn't that right, darling?"

"Absolutely," Natalie had answered. What else could she have said, with her husband and a complete stranger beaming at her as if she were some clever new wind-up doll?

Natalie brushed her teeth, rinsed her mouth, and winced when she looked up and saw a universe of Natalies watching her.

"Ugh," she said to the straggly hair, the pale face, the smudge of mascara beneath one eye that was all that remained of the makeup she'd never taken off last night. She could have: the guest suite was well-equipped. The designer had seen to that. Cotton sheets so soft they felt like silk, Unisex pajamas, fluffy white bathrobes, disposable slippers, sample sizes of cosmetics enough to stock a department store. Hairbrush, comb, toothbrushes, toothpaste, mouthwash, tissues... The man with the flutey voice had thought of everything. And when they had guests, part of Luz's housekeeping duties was to restock whatever had been used.

The only thing the decorator hadn't thought of was how a woman was supposed to feel when she awoke in the guest room because she'd told her husband of ten years that she wanted a divorce.

Natalie turned off the water and patted her face briskly with a towel. She hadn't planned to say the words, not consciously. Not last night, certainly. But, really, she was glad she had. It was better this way. Why prolong things? She'd known, for a long time, that the marriage was over. That she and Gage were living a charade, known since she'd lost the baby—a baby, she'd realized, he'd never really wanted—that he didn't love her anymore, that she didn't love him. That—that—

"Oh, Gage," Natalie whispered, and sank down in the middle of the tiled floor. "Gage," she said again, her voice breaking, and she buried her face in her hands and wept until she was sure she could never weep again.

And, after that, she wept some more.

Gage awakened, as always, promptly at 6:00 a.m.

It was the habit of a lifetime, one he'd developed in those long-ago years when he'd first headed east from Texas. He'd figured out really early that a twenty-one-year-old kid with half a college degree, no discernible skills in much of anything that didn't involve a horse, and a brand-new wife to support had to work hard at being an early bird if he was going to catch even the smallest of worms.

It wasn't necessary now, of course. His offices didn't open until nine but still, every morning, rain or shine, he was out of bed at six on the button.

Usually, he crept around quietly in the shadowy darkness with the bedroom blinds shut, doing his damnedest not to disturb Natalie. She always said she didn't mind, that what she called her internal clock was still set at dawn.

But he'd vowed, a long time ago, that his wife would never have to creep out of a warm bed at dawn again. No way would he ever have to watch Natalie stumble into her clothes, then go off to a day spent waiting tables.

He could remember the time he'd told her that.

"I'll take you up on the no-waiting-tables deal," Natalie had said, laughing. Then she'd thrown her arms around his neck and flashed a sexy smile. "Come to think of it, staying in bed is a pretty fine idea, too... As long as you stay there to keep me occupied."

"Occupied?" he'd said, with a puzzled look that was hard to maintain because just the light brush of Natalie's body against his had always been enough to make him go crazy.

"Occupied," she'd said, and then she'd threaded her hands into his hair, drawn his head down to hers, kissed him with her mouth open so that he could taste her honeyed warmth...

Gage's face hardened.

Kissed him, exactly as she had last night, just before she'd said, "Gage, I want a divorce."

He muttered an oath, kicked the afghan blanket from his legs, and sat up.

"Ouch."

So much for spending the night on the leather couch in the den. Gage groaned, pressed his hands to the small of his back, and rose to his feet.

Leather couches were not made for sleeping. Neither was this room. It was too big, too impersonal, too filled with stuff. What man would want to share his sleeping quarters with a pool table?

Not him, that was for sure. But Natalie had stalked off to the guest suite, leaving the bedroom to him.

"You can have it," she'd said with dramatic flair.

Gage groaned again as he hobbled across the hall to the downstairs lavatory. He could have it, but he hadn't wanted it. That huge room, with its enormous bed, all to himself? With Natalie's perfume and a thousand memories lingering in the air?

"No way," he muttered as he splashed cold water on his face.

A man didn't want to spend the first night of the rest of his life surrounded by reminders of what he was leaving behind.

Gage took a towel from the rack and scrubbed it over his face. Towel? That was a laugh. These puny things were more like handkerchiefs. But Natalie liked them. Natalie and that fruity designer, the one who'd hand-picked the leather couch Gage had thought, until last night, was only uncomfortable to sit on.

He looked into the mirror. A guy in a dress shirt and rumpled black trousers with a satin stripe down the side looked back at him. Hell, he was a mess. Hair uncombed, face unshaven…he looked like Chewbacca after a bad night, but what could you expect after six hours on a cowhide-covered rack?

A smile. Damn, yes. A smile, at the very least. Because now, if nothing else, he'd had his life handed back to him.

Gage stomped down the hall and up the curving staircase to the master bedroom.

Okay, maybe he hadn't seen it that way, at first. Natalie's announcement had been...upsetting.

Upsetting?

He shot an unforgiving glance down the corridor, towards the guest room and its closed door, where Natalie was still sleeping the sleep of what he supposed she thought of as the innocent and martyred.

"Let's be honest here," he muttered as he marched through the master bedroom and into the bathroom.

I want a divorce weren't exactly the words a man expected to hear from his wife, especially after they'd been going at each other like two teenagers in hormonal overdrive...

Like the two teenagers they'd once been.

Pictures flashed through his head. He and Natalie, parked in his car on Superstition Butte. Natalie, her beautiful face pink and glowing after their first kiss. Natalie, crying out in passion in his arms.

Gage swallowed hard, slammed the bathroom door shut, and pulled off what remained of his rumpled monkey suit.

Sex. That was all it had been, all it had ever been. His father had tried to tell him that. His brothers, too. Well, no. Not Travis. By then, Travis had already taken off for parts unknown. But Slade had tried to make him listen to reason, and Gage had waved off his kid brother's warnings, laughed them off, really, telling Slade he was too young to understand love, telling his father he was too jaded to understand it.

And now, it was over.

Oh, the heat was still there. For all he knew, it always would be. Natalie was a beautiful, sexy woman. Why pretend otherwise? And he was a man who had an eye for beauty.

Gage glanced at the ornate gold and platinum faucets jutting from the marble sink. Well, for some kinds of beauty. Not stuff like this. He shuddered. This was ugly. But Natalie liked it, the same as she liked the Spanish Inquisition couch.

"All to madam's tastes, Mr. Baron," the obsequious little interior decorator had explained any time he'd questioned a purchase.

All of which proved, Gage thought glumly as he stepped into the shower, all of which most definitely proved how little he and Natalie suited each other.

That was why her announcement last night really hadn't come as such a shock. Well, it had, at first. He'd felt as if the ground were dissolving under his feet when she'd looked at him, her eyes cold, and said, "Gage, I want a divorce."

"A divorce?" he'd repeated dumbly, as if saying the word might give it some real meaning, turn it into one he could understand.

"Yes," she'd said. "A divorce."

And then a bunch of the Holcombs's guests had come traipsing through the garden, talking and laughing.

What's the matter with you people? he'd wanted to shout. Don't you realize that the whole world just stopped?

But he hadn't said anything, partly because his brain seemed to have gone numb, partly because Natalie had swung away from him and was hurrying towards the gate that led to the beach. He'd gone after her, following as she made her way not to the sea but around the side of the mansion, up the walkway, to the front of the house.

She'd taken the long way. Evidently, she hadn't been any more interested in pasting on a smile and saying good-night to a bunch of people than he was.

She was already heading for the street by the time he got to the driveway.

"My car," he said to the kid with the pimples, pulling out the first bill from his pocket. "And make it quick."

It must have been a hefty tip because the kid took off like a rocket and delivered the car thirty seconds later.

"Thank you, sir," he said, but Gage was already in the Vette, pulling away, tires screaming as he raced after Natalie.

He slowed when he caught up to her and put down his window.

"Get in the car."

She ignored him.

"Get in the damn car," he said, and something in his voice must have warned her that he was in no mood for games because she'd stopped, wrenched open the door and climbed in.

"What does 'I want a divorce' mean?" he'd growled.

"It's not Swahili, Gage. It means exactly what you think it means," Natalie had replied without looking at him, and she'd sat silent as a statue all the way back to their house, where he'd roared up the driveway and come to a screeching, bone-jarring stop. She was out of the car, into the house, up the stairs in one fluid motion, with him hot on her heels.

"Natalie," he'd said, "what's going on here?"

But it was a pointless question. For starters, she didn't answer it. And even a man as dumb as he could see what was going on here.

Natalie had marched towards the guest suite, not towards the bedroom.

"Where do you think you're going?" he'd yelled.

She hadn't answered that, either, and he'd felt his blood pressure zoom up the scale as the guest room door slammed behind her and the sound of the lock sliding home echoed like a rifle shot through the silent house.

So he'd stood there, hands balled into fists, brows tied in a knot, while the adrenaline pumped through his body at a thousand gallons a minute. Should he go after her? Demand answers? Should he break down the guest room door, break it down and...

And what?

He'd never felt more useless, more frustrated, more furious in his whole life.

And, short of doing something he knew he'd regret later, there wasn't a thing he could do about it.

Except not sleep in the master bedroom.

It wasn't much, but it was something—something, it turned out, that had come close to breaking his back.

Well, at least it had given him time to think.

Gage shut off the shower, stepped out and strode into the bedroom with a towel tied around his waist.

Natalie wanted out? Fine. So did he. Wasn't that exactly what he'd been thinking while he'd dressed for the party last night?

What they'd had, what he'd thought they had, just wasn't there anymore. The truth was, they quarreled all the time. Over everything. Natalie didn't hurry to the door when he came home. Hell, most of the time she wasn't even there when he came home, not even after he'd busted his tail flying through five time zones to get to her, the way he'd done a couple of weeks ago after he'd opened the newest Baron's in Samoa, where he'd had to grin like an idiot while some broad with too many teeth and not enough clothes had propped her boobs against his arm.

"Miss South Pacific," the hotel manager had hissed into his ear. "It's good for local business."

And it would have been good as a little joke to share with Natalie. But the days of shared jokes and smiles were long gone.

Oh, she could still turn him on. There was no question about that. Gage reached into his closet, then stopped.

Except, now that he thought about it, even sex hadn't been the same lately. There were the nights he thought about reaching for Natalie in bed, but didn't do it. He was tired. She was tired. But hadn't there been a time he hadn't thought about reaching for her, a time he'd just done it? And, after they'd made love, hadn't there been a time he'd never had to wonder if Natalie had—if she'd—

Gage grabbed for a shirt, a tie, a suit.

What did any of it matter? Last night, tossing on that couch, he'd admitted to himself that she had simply spoken the truth before he had. Their marriage had run its course. Marriages did that in his family. Just look at his old man, tucked in with wife number five. Just look at Travis, one down and swearing he'd never get trapped again.

Gage snorted.

And then there was Slade, who worked at staying single.

And Caitlin…well, forget Caitlin. Not because she wasn't really a Baron by blood but because his stepsister was too smart to even consider becoming a participant in the marriage wars.

Gage stepped into his briefs, pulled on his trousers and zipped them up.

Yessirree, today was the first day of the rest of his life. A life without a wife who'd made it clearer and clearer she didn't love him.

She had, once. He knew she had. Maybe—maybe, if they hadn't lost the baby…

His face hardened. The baby had nothing to do with it. Natalie hadn't really wanted a baby, anyway. He knew that, now. That was something else it was time he admitted.

"Okay," he said aloud. "It's over. And I'm damn glad it is."

"So am I," Natalie said, and Gage whirled around to face her. His face reddened.

"I didn't know you were there."

"So I gather."

"I didn't mean—"

"Didn't you?"

The coldness in her face was like a blow to the heart. Gage's mouth thinned.

"Did you want something?" he asked politely.

"No. I mean, yes. I mean…"

What *did* she mean? If only she hadn't stumbled in without knocking. If only she hadn't heard him say those words. He was right, of course. It was over and, dammit, she was as relieved as he was. Only—only he didn't have to sound so happy…

"Natalie?"

She blinked. Gage had come closer. All she had to do was reach out her hand to touch him…

"Natalie? Are you all right?"

She swallowed hard and nodded.

"I'm fine. I'm sorry I barged in on you, Gage. I should have knocked, but the door was open."

"Don't be ridiculous. You don't have to—"

"You're busy. I'll wait until you're finished and then I'll—"

"No." The word shot from his throat. "No," he said carefully, and ran his fingers through his hair. "I'm not busy at all. I'm just getting dressed."

Yes. She could see that for herself. He was wearing nothing but a pair of gray trousers, zipped but open at the waist so that they drooped low on his hips. And he'd just come from the shower. His dark hair was still damp and uncombed. It lay over his forehead in a way that made her want to go to him and push it back.

Habit, she thought, and stood straighter. It was habit, too, that made her gaze drop lower, to survey that familiar body. The broad shoulders. The muscled arms and chest. The narrow waist that tapered to long legs...

Her gaze shot back to his face.

"That's—that's all right." She cleared her throat. "I'll wait."

"Natalie." His hand fell on her shoulder as she turned away. "Did you, uh, did you want something?"

"My clothes." She made a little gesture that took in the white robe, hanging almost to her toes. "I need my clothes."

"Oh." He nodded. "I, ah, I thought you might have wanted to talk."

"About what?"

About what? Gage's vision clouded. How could she ask that? How could she sound so damned polite?

"About us," he said tightly. "That's what I thought you might want to talk about."

She nodded. "I don't think there's anything to say," she said quietly. "We both know our marriage is over. We've known it for a long time. I just finally put it into words last night."

A muscle knotted in Gage's jaw. "Of course," he said politely. "You're right. Now that I've had time to think it over, I know that."

Natalie forced a smile to her lips. "I just...I'm not sure what we're supposed to do next."

"No. Neither am I." He walked to the bed, where he'd dropped the rest of the clothes he'd taken from the closet. "Talk to a lawyer, I guess."

"A lawyer." Natalie stumbled a little over the word. "Yes. Yes, of course. Do we use one or do we use two?"

"Two," Gage said in that same polite tone. He slipped on his shirt, began doing up the buttons. "Why don't you call Jim Rutherford?"

"I assumed you'd want Jim."

Gage shook his head. "That's okay. You might as well deal with somebody you know. I'll get someone else."

"Yes, but…" God, what was wrong with her? What did she care what lawyer he used? His feelings weren't her problem, not anymore.

"Landon. Grant Landon."

"Who?"

The name from the past had tumbled from Gage's lips without warning but now that it had, he knew it made sense. A friend. A real friend, one who'd known him in that long-ago time when he'd stood halfway between the defiance of his abandoned youth and the promise of the man he was to become.

"You met him in New York. I brought him by a couple of times when I was in law school. Remember?"

Did she remember? Natalie almost laughed, or maybe she almost cried. She'd never forget New York. Gage in school, at class all day, bent over his books half the night. She, working at the restaurant where the grease on the griddle probably dated back to pre-history. The little walk-up apartment on Eighth Street, where the water always gurgled in the pipes and the thin walls that transmitted every sound from the apartment next door.

And the joy. The happiness. The wonder of being Gage's wife, of being able to begin each day seeing his face, of ending each night wrapped in his arms…

"Nat?"

She looked up, her vision hazed by tears. Gage had come

closer. He was only a breath away. He smiled and lay his
hand lightly against her cheek.

"Do you remember New York, Nat?" he said.

Natalie stared at him. Oh, he was so transparent. Did he
think he could do this forever? A soft word. A smile. A gentle
touch. And she was supposed to succumb, to go into his arms,
to pretend that she meant more to him than an ornament.
Because that was all she was. An ornament. One he could
drape with jewels and place in a glowing setting.

Once, she'd been a woman of flesh and blood. Gage's wife.
A whole person, the one he discussed things with. Planned
with. Chose to be with, above and beyond anyone else, instead of jetting off at every opportunity to meet with
Important People, to be photographed at the opening of the
latest Baron resort with some nubile young thing breathing
down his neck, Miss Samoa or Miss Pittsburgh or—or Miss
Minnie Mouse, for all she knew or cared...

Natalie jerked back.

"I remember," she said coldly. "That ratty apartment. The
water that shook the pipes. The noise from next door, and the
stink of old grease in my hair. You're damned right, I remember. How could I ever forget?"

Gage's eyes went flat.

"I see. The bell rings for round one."

"And what's that supposed to mean?"

His smile was tight and unpleasant. "Come on, babe, don't
give me that innocent look. Half your girlfriends have been
divorced. Round one, in which the much-put-upon little
woman lays out a list of all the sacrifices she's made for
hubby."

Natalie's chin lifted. "What an excellent idea," she said
sweetly. "I'll be sure to mention it to Jim."

"And I'll be sure to tell Grant that he'd better help me
figure out a way to lock up the valuables."

"You do that," Natalie said through her teeth.

"Damn right," Gage said through his. "Now, was there
anything else you wanted, or can I finish getting dressed in
the privacy of my own room?"

Natalie fluttered her lashes. "Your own room?" She looked around slowly, then at Gage again. "Your own room, my dear, almost-ex-husband, is waiting for you at your club. Or at your hotel. One of your hotels, anyway." Her smile glittered. "But it certainly isn't here. As you so carefully pointed out, this is round one. That means the house is the least of what I expect to get."

Gage slapped his hands on his hips.

"You're joking."

Natalie slapped her hands on her hips, too. "Do I look as if I'm joking?"

His eyes narrowed. "It'll take a court order to get me out of here, babe."

"I'm sure Jim will provide me with one."

Natalie turned away from him and sauntered towards the door. It was crazy, but the sight of that stiff, slender back sent Gage's blood pressure soaring again.

"And I'm sure Grant will know what you can do with your court order," he said, his voice rising.

She swung to face him, her hand on the doorknob. "I hope so," she said politely. "I hope, too, that your Mister...Landon? I hope he's able to do such things, here in Florida."

Gage blinked. "What?"

"He practices in New York. Isn't that what you said? And this is Florida. I just hope, for both our sakes, your dear old pal can hang out his shingle in another state because I'm telling you right now, Gage, I don't want this thing dragging on forever."

Gage strode towards her. "It won't. Oh, it won't." He grabbed Natalie's shoulders, drew her up to her toes, lowered his face until they were nose to nose. "Because I'm telling you right now, babe, you can forget about a divorce."

Natalie turned white. "But you just said..."

"I know what I said!" He let go of her, yanked open the door, and she stumbled backwards into the hall. "I know exactly what I said, dammit." He slammed the door shut and glared at it. "And I meant every word," he muttered. "Every mother-loving word."

Enraged, he kicked the wall, welcomed the sharp pain the thoughtless action sent shooting through his bare toes.

"Every word," he said, and buried his face in his hands.

CHAPTER THREE

GAGE pushed open the double glass doors that led to the main offices of Baron Resorts. Carol, seated behind the reception desk, gave him her usual sunny smile over the mug of steaming coffee she held in her hands.

"Morning, Mr. Baron."

Gage glared at her.

"It's after nine," he snapped. "You're supposed to be working."

Carol's smile faded. "I am working. I mean, I'm just—"

"You want coffee, wait until your break." Gage marched past her. "Let's have a little efficiency around here, if you don't mind."

"No, Mr. Baron. I mean, yes, Mr. Baron. I mean—"

He pushed his way through the next set of doors and strode towards his office. His secretary rose to her feet as he swept past her desk.

"Good morning, Mr. Baron. Mr. Folger called. Mr. Okada, too. And there are several faxes from—"

"No calls," he snapped. "No faxes. No interruptions. Understood?"

Rosa's dark brows lifted. "Certainly, sir. No interruptions. But—"

Gage swung towards her. "What part of the word 'no' don't you understand?"

Color flooded Rosa's face. "No part of it, sir."

"Good. Then don't disturb me for anything less than a five-alarm fire or an armed insurrection."

He slammed his office door shut, tossed his briefcase on a low beechwood table...

"Hell," he muttered, and opened the door again. "Rosa?"

Rosa looked up from her computer keyboard. "Yes, sir?"

Her tone was polite but stiff, and her cheeks were still red. Gage sighed and walked towards her.

"I apologize. I didn't mean to take your head off. It's just…" *Just what, Baron? Just that your wife is leaving you?* "It's just that, ah, that I had a late night."

Rosa smiled. "I can imagine."

"Sorry?"

"The Holcombs's party. According to today's paper, it was a smashing success."

"Oh. Uh, yeah. Yeah, it was—terrific."

"I'll hold all your calls, Mr. Baron."

"Thanks. And do me a favor, please. Tell Carol to call Starbuck's, order herself a couple of pounds of whatever coffee she likes and charge it to me. And tell her I said she can keep a pot of the stuff at her elbow all day long, if that's what she wants."

"Sir?"

"Just tell her what I said, okay? She'll understand."

"I'll tell her. And I'll see to it you're not disturbed—but there is this one envelope that arrived by messenger this morning…"

Gage sighed and held out his hand. "Okay, okay. Hand it over, though why you'd think something that comes via Express Mail would be…" He frowned as Rosa put the heavy vellum envelope in his hand. "This didn't come Express Mail."

"No, sir. It was hand-delivered, as I said."

He looked at the cream-colored envelope. His name and address had been written in flowing, elegant script.

"It's quite impressive, sir."

"It is, indeed." He grinned. "Probably an advertising gimmick. 'Come in and test drive our newest super-duper, ultra-luxurious boatmobile.' Something like that."

Rosa laughed. "I'm sure you're right, Mr. Baron. But I thought it might be important."

"Sure. No need to explain." Gage smiled. "Just do me a favor and hold everything else, okay? I have some, ah, some thinking I want to do about, ah, about that property in Puerto Rico.''

"Certainly, sir."

His smile held until he'd shut the door to his office. Then it slid from his face like the mask it was.

"Great job, Baron," he muttered as he dropped the vellum envelope on his desk. "First you chop off the heads of two of the best people in your office, then you stand there and sputter excuses as if you were a ten-year-old explaining how the ball broke the window." He yanked off his jacket, loosened his tie, kicked back his swivel chair and collapsed into it. "Next thing you know, you'll be phoning one of those talk show shrinks and whining out your tale of woe to a million people."

What tale of woe? His marriage was breaking up. Well, so what? Divorce had been a part of his childhood. Back then, only his brothers, and then Caitlin, had understood. Now— now, it was an everyday thing.

Enough of feeling sorry for himself. He needed to think about something else. Clear his head, so he could approach things logically. Today was a business day, same as any other. He had appointments, meetings, probably a lunch scheduled with somebody or other.

The ever-efficient Rosa had centered his appointment book, open, on his desk. A neat stack of faxes lay to its left. To the right were half a dozen "while you were out" memos.

The vellum envelope had landed on top of them.

Gage pushed it aside, picked up the memos and leafed through them. Words ran together in a senseless pattern. He frowned, dumped the memos in the wastebasket and reached for the faxes, but he couldn't get past the first sentence on any of them.

"Damn," he said, and dropped them, too.

How was he supposed to keep his mind on work? How was he supposed to concentrate on anything but what was happening in his personal life?

He shoved back his chair, got to his feet and drew open the vertical blinds that covered the wall of glass behind him.

Below, sun-worshiping guests lazed around the Windsong's pool, which had been designed in the spirit of a lazy river, complete with waterfalls that flowed over hidden grottoes. Beyond, a stretch of white sand led to the emerald sea.

Everything he'd busted his tail to create was out there. Well, there and beyond, in a dozen places around the globe. Under his command, the sorry excuse for a hotel he'd almost hocked his soul to buy had become a world-famous, five-star resort, the center of what the financial wizards had taken to calling Baron's Kingdom.

He was a successful, happy man.

At least, he had been, until last night.

Gage sank down into his chair again, propped his elbows on the desk and held his head.

What to do? What to do?

There had to be a way around this. Two people didn't just walk away from a marriage after they'd invested ten years of their lives in it.

It wasn't logical. Wasn't practical. It was pointless and wasteful and foolish. Okay. He'd tell Natalie that, give her the chance to change her mind...

Was he crazy? Give her the chance to cut him to shreds again, was more like it. Besides, he wanted out. How come he kept forgetting that?

He muttered an oath, a creative one dredged up from those long-ago days when he'd worked with his hands, not with his head.

"Got to keep busy," he muttered, "got to stop thinking."

His gaze fell on the vellum envelope. Okay, even reading a hokey ad for an overpriced car or maybe a boat, considering that this was Florida, might be good for a distraction.

He ripped open the envelope flap, extracted a heavy formal notecard. His brows rose as he read it.

Your presence is requested at
The eighty-fifth birthday celebration
Of Mr. Jonas Baron
Saturday and Sunday, June the 14th and 15th

At the Baron Ranch
'Espada'
Brazos Springs, Texas
R.S.V.P.

A note was scrawled beneath the perfectly executed calligraphy.

"Gage," it read, "you'd damn well better come if you know what's good for you. No excuses, you hear?"

The brusque words were followed by a bold capital C— and softened with the drawing of a tiny heart.

A grin spread across Gage's face. Catie never changed. Tough as nails on the outside, soft and sweet inside, though she'd probably have slugged him if he'd ever dared say something like that to her face.

His grin faded.

Now his morning was perfect. First the confrontation with Natalie and now this demand that he attend a command performance at Espada. Oh, yeah. Today was shaping up to be a gem.

Jonas, pushing eighty-five. Was it really possible? He hadn't seen his father in a year. Two, maybe. But in his mind's eye, Jonas was ageless, with a body as tough and straight as an ironwood tree and silver eyes that could stare down a hawk.

He put down the vellum card. Eighty-five. That was quite a number. Well, he'd have to phone on the—what day was it, anyway? The fourteenth of June? The fifteenth? Either way, he'd call the ranch, wish the old man a happy birthday. And send him a gift, of course, though what you could send a man who had everything he wanted and disdained everything else was beyond him.

Gage's expression softened. He'd make a separate call, to Caitlin. Explain that, much as he wanted to, he couldn't possibly break away and—

His private phone rang. The sound startled him. No one had that number except—

"Baby," he said, grabbing the phone. "Natalie, I love you so—"

"And I love you, too, precious," a falsetto voice warbled, "but my husband's starting to get suspicious."

Gage jerked upright in his chair. "Travis? Trav, is that you?"

A deep, masculine chuckle sounded over the line. "I know it's probably disappointing as all get-out but yeah, it's me. Good morning."

A slow smile spread across Gage's lips.

"Good morning?" He glanced at his watch and gave a soft whistle. "My, oh, my, I am impressed, Travis. Why, it's hardly seven o'clock, your time. I didn't think you West Coast big shots turned over in bed until us hardworkin' Easterners were darned near havin' lunch."

"I already told him that," another deep, lazy voice said.

Gage's smile became a grin. "Slade?"

"The one and only," Slade Baron replied.

"Hell, I don't believe this! What are you two guys doin'? Havin' a reunion out there in Malibu? Or are you both in Boston, livin' it up in that big old house on Beacon Hill my little brother calls home?"

"I'm in Boston," Slade said.

"And I'm in Malibu," Travis said. "This three-way brotherly phone call is comin' to you courtesy of the marvels of modern-day science."

"I'll bet it's the only three-way ever been done by telephone," Slade said with a wicked grin at the pretty young secretary who'd just brought him his coffee. "Thank you, darlin'."

"Don't you 'darlin'' me, pal," Travis said with a mock growl, "or I'll fly straight to that fancy-pants mansion of yours and beat you up the way I used to when you were a scrawny twelve-year-old and I was a strappin' lad of thirteen."

"Uh-huh. You an' who else?"

"Me an' my man Gage. Isn't that right, Gage?" Travis

chuckled. "'Course, it'll have to wait until the sun gets up in the sky a piece, so my brain starts workin' right."

All three brothers laughed. Gage could have sworn he felt that laughter reach out over the miles and enfold him in its warmth.

It never failed to amaze him, how easily they all fell into the teasing repartee of childhood. Months went by now without their seeing each other but it didn't matter. The small battles they'd fought as kids didn't matter, either. Put two of them together in a room—or on a telephone line—and the memories flooded back. Put three of them together and it was as if the years had fallen away. Even their accents changed and took on the soft, drawling cadence of their growing-up years in Texas, until Travis finally cleared his throat and got down to the reason for the call.

"Okay, guys," he said, and sighed. "I wish to hell we could avoid the topic and I'm sure you do, too, but it's time for a reality check."

"The invitation," Slade said.

Gage heard the rustle of paper over the line. "You got yours, too?"

"This morning, bright and early. Trav?"

"Bright and early is right. Mine arrived at six."

Slade laughed. "And interrupted you and a guest."

"Go on," Travis hesitated. "Let's just say I was otherwise involved when I got this invitation."

"What a tough life he leads," Slade drawled.

"I'd expect some compassion from you, kid," Travis said. "Not from Gage, of course, since he gave up his freedom years ago." His voice softened. "How's my girl, by the way? You still treating her right, or is she about ready to use that pretty head of hers and ditch you for me?"

Gage's smile faded. "She's fine," he said tightly, and knew he'd made a mistake the minute he heard the overwhelming silence humming across the lines.

"Gage?" Slade said. "You okay?"

"Yeah," Travis said. "Is everything all right?"

"Yes."

"You sure? Because you don't sound—"

"Listen, maybe you two guys can horse around all day," Gage said, even more tightly, "but I've got things to do. So let's get down to it, okay?"

There was the sound of throat-clearing on both coasts. "Right," Slade said. "Uh, business. Well, Travis already put the agenda on the table. What are we going to do about this command performance the old man's got planned for the middle of the month?"

"Ignore it," Gage said firmly. "I've got—"

"Things to do," Travis said. "Yeah, I heard that. And believe me, I don't have any greater desire to go back to Espada for a dress rehearsal of *King Lear* than either of you guys, but—"

"Lear?" Slade said, sounding puzzled. "Hey, this is Texas we're talking about, not Stratford-on-Avon."

"Come on, Slade, give me a break. You know what this is all about. Jonas is starting to feel mortal."

"Jonas?" Slade snorted. "Our father's got every intention of making it to one hundred and you know what? My money's on him."

"Mine, too. But I suspect the old boy's looking around, taking stock of that little spread of seven zillion acres he calls home, sweet home, and figuring it's time he made plans on how to divvy up the kingdom."

"Well, I don't need to spend a miserable weekend listening to him snap out orders to know that I don't give a damn how he does it." Gage rose from his chair, paced to the door, opened it and mimed that he was drinking a cup of coffee to Rosa, who nodded and slipped out from behind her desk. "I'll send a gift, phone the ranch, wish Jonas the best..." He smiled his thanks as Rosa handed him a cup. "You two guys can enjoy the party without me," he finished as he sat down at his desk again.

"Hold it right there, pal." Slade's voice rang with indignation. "I never said I was going. In fact, I'm going to be in Baltimore that weekend."

"Or in the Antarctic," Travis said lazily. "Anywhere it takes to avoid this shindig, right?"

"Wrong. I've put in the past eight weeks on plans for a new bank in Baltimore, and I'll be damned if—"

"Easy does it, Slade. I was just kidding."

Slade sighed. "And I was lying through my teeth. Not about the commission, but about why I can't make it to Espada."

"Amazing," Gage said softly. "Here we are, three grown men, all of us falling over our own feet in a rush to keep clear of the place where we grew up."

"Some people call the place where they grew up 'home,'" Slade said, trying for a light touch but coming up short.

"Yeah," Travis said, trying for the same light touch, "but they aren't the sons of Jonas Baron."

"The Sons of Jonas Baron," Gage said, trying even harder. "Sounds like a movie."

"Not a bad idea," Slade said. "I can play myself but they'd need to hire stand-ins for you two. Splash those ugly mugs of yours across the big screen and they'd scare away paying customers."

This time, at last, they all laughed.

"The thing is," said Travis, "tough as the old man is, eighty-five is a pretty impressive number."

"So?" Bitterness tinged Gage's voice. "I don't much remember him being impressed enough by other numbers. Your eighteenth birthday, for instance. Or when Slade finished his two years of grad school."

"Or your big fifth anniversary party," Travis said, and Gage felt the pain of Natalie's announcement rip through him again. "But, what the hell, gentlemen, we're bigger than that, right?"

Groans greeted the announcement, but Travis was undeterred.

"Well, we are. We're young, he's old. That's a simple fact." His voice softened. "And then there's Caitlin."

"Yeah." Slade sighed. "I do hate to disappoint her."

"Disappoint her?" Gage muttered. "Hell, Catie'll come after us and cut out our hearts when she hears we're not coming."

"Or other, even more important parts of our anatomies," Slade said.

The three Barons laughed, and then Gage gave a deep sigh.

"Yeah, I know. I don't like letting her down, but I don't see a choice here, guys. I'm sorry, but I don't."

"The choice," Travis said in the tone of reason that had made him such a successful attorney, "the choice, my man, is that there is no choice. We have to show up at this thing."

"No way," two voices said in unison.

"Look, we're not kids anymore. Jonas can't get under our skin. He can't make us miserable and, what the hell, we do owe him a show of respect. And think how happy we can make Caitlin by showing our faces, singing 'Happy Birthday' or whatever it is she's got planned, before we head out to the real world again. What'll it take? A couple of days? That's not much, when you come down to it, is it?"

Silence skimmed along the phone line. "Maybe not," Slade said after a while.

Maybe not, Gage thought—but the birthday weekend was only ten days away. Every instinct he possessed told him it was going to take longer than that to fix this mess with Natalie, to convince her that he still loved her, that he wanted her because, dammit, he did.

"Okay," Slade said, and heaved a sigh. "I'm in."

"Great," Travis said. "Gage?"

Gage cleared his throat. "I can't."

"Dammit, Gage, if Slade can, and I can—"

"I can't, I'm telling you! I've got—I have things to take care of. Important things."

"It's just a weekend," Slade said.

"Well, I don't have a weekend to spare."

"Listen here, brother," Travis snapped. "If I can manage the time and Slade can manage the time—"

"Good," Gage snarled. "Great. I'm proud of the two of

you. But I'm busy. Too busy for this kind of nonsense. I have some sensitive things going on here. You guys understand that, or do I have to put it on a billboard?''

He heard the harshness, the anger, of his own words echoing around him. His brothers were silent and he shut his eyes and put his fist to his forehead. He could almost see the looks they'd be sending each other if they were in the same room.

He took a deep breath.

"I'm sorry," he said, his voice near a whisper. "But I can't be there. I just can't."

"Sure," Travis said after a minute.

"Understood," Slade said a beat later. "Well…"

There was silence, then the sound of a throat being cleared. "Well," three voices said at one time, and then there were hurried goodbyes, good wishes…

The phone went dead. Gage sat staring at it, waiting—and smiled a little when it rang.

"Listen," Travis said without bothering to say hello. "If there's a problem on your end…"

"I'm okay."

"Yeah, sure you are, but if there should be a problem, whatever—"

"I'll call you," Gage said quietly.

"Yeah," Travis said, cleared his throat, and hung up. The phone rang again, almost immediately.

"Gage?"

Gage sighed. "Yes, Slade."

"Look, if you, ah, if you need anything—"

"I'm fine."

"Yeah, sure, but if you should need anything, somebody to talk to, whatever—"

"I'll call you," Gage said softly.

"Right." Slade cleared his throat and hung up.

Slowly, Gage put down the telephone. He forgot, sometimes, what it was like, having a family that loved you. Maybe Natalie had forgotten, too. He was her family, after all, just as she was his. Maybe all she needed was for him to sit her down, tell her how he loved her...

The phone rang again. Gage rolled his eyes and picked it up.

"Listen, you guys, I swear to you, I'm perfectly fine. There's not a thing troubling me. You got that? My life is perfect. I'm just too busy to take time out for a weekend of sentimental claptrap."

"You don't have to convince me," Natalie said. "I know all about how busy you are, Gage."

"Natalie?" He shot to his feet. "I didn't realize—"

"No," she said, her voice trembling. "No, you never did. I just hope you're not too busy to take down this phone number."

"What phone number? Nat, listen—"

"My phone number. I've left you, Gage. I took an apartment off Lincoln Drive."

"Huh?" Gage ran his hand through his hair. "But the last thing you said this morning was—"

"I changed my mind."

"Natalie, baby—"

"And I've spoken with Jim Rutherford. I think you should speak with your attorney, too."

Gage's eyes narrowed. "All this," he said slowly, "in one morning?"

"All this, in one morning."

"How long have you been planning this, Natalie?"

"I haven't. I've thought about it, but—"

"Thought about leaving me? *Thought* about it?"

He shut his eyes, remembering the nights she'd feigned sleep, the times he'd taken her in his arms anyway and felt as if she were made of wood. Was that when she'd thought about leaving him? When she lay beside him, when she lay beneath him, in the darkness?

"Well," he said, his voice a growl, his heart trying to break and harden at the same time, "I've got news for you, baby. I thought about it, too. For months. I just didn't know how to tell you but I can see, I needn't have worried."

Natalie put the back of her hand to her mouth, biting hard on her knuckles so she wouldn't give this man she'd once loved the satisfaction of hearing her weep. "If you don't know how to swim, don't jump into the deep end," Liz Holcomb had pleaded after Natalie had poured out her heart over endless cups of black coffee. "Oh, Natalie, don't do anything too quickly. Wait. Think. Give it time."

But she had waited, for what seemed years and years. She'd waited for her husband to look up and notice that he'd forgotten who she was, that she was at least as important as his hotels, his meetings, his money.

And then she'd looked at him in the Holcombs's garden last night and she'd realized that the only thing Gage wanted from her anymore was what she could give him in bed.

The knowledge had broken her heart, but it had given her the resolve she'd needed to turn her life around.

So she'd called Jim Rutherford, phoned a rental agent because, despite the threat she'd made, there wasn't a way in the world she wanted to stay in that house. She'd done everything she had to do...and all the while she'd hoped that maybe, just maybe, a miracle might happen. Gage might suddenly see how serious this was, how much they each were going to lose when they lost each other.

"Natalie," he'd say, "don't leave me. I love you, I've never stopped loving you..."

"Actually," he said coldly, "I'm glad the charade's finally over."

Yes," Natalie whispered. She swiped the back of her hand at the tears that were streaming down her face. "So am I. It's—it's good that we've both decided to be honest about what we want."

"Out," Gage snarled. "That's what I want." He slammed down the phone, snatched it up again and dialed Slade's number. "Slade? I've changed my mind. I'll be at Espada for Jonas's birthday party. Yeah, well, I just—I shifted things around, that's all. Do me a favor, call Travis and let him know. Oh, absolutely. We'll have a blast. Uh-huh. Just like old times."

Just like old times, Gage thought bitterly as he hung up the phone.

And wasn't that one hell of a thing to be looking forward to?

CHAPTER FOUR

GAGE was beginning to look forward to his father's birthday party.

Going back to Espada, visiting with Caitlin and his brothers, seeing old friends, would be fun. It might even be okay, seeing the old man again. Jonas was tough to get along with but he was definitely an interesting character.

And he had Natalie to thank for making his choice an easy one.

He hadn't heard a word from her recently. The silence, as his old man used to say about some of his ex-wives, was deafening.

Like father, like son, Gage thought as he tossed a handful of T-shirts into the suitcase. His father certainly knew all about divorce.

Gage's lips compressed into a tight smile. He and the old man had never had much in common except half a set of chromosomes. Well, now they'd have something more. Jonas could look down that eagle beak of his, go into his "I told you so" routine and say, "Didn't I tell you not to marry that girl, boy?"

Oh, yeah. The two of them could have a long heart-to-heart now, and wasn't that a winner of a thought?

Gage dumped a bathing suit into the suitcase. He'd need it, for the pool, but maybe he and Slade and Travis could ride out to the creek the way they used to, when they were kids, and go skinny-dipping. The memory turned his smile into a real one. Skinny-dipping, and then, when they got older, sitting on the red rocks above the creek, still naked as jaybirds, popping the beers they'd chilled in the water, telling each other tall tales and maybe even some truths.

It was going to be one hell of a weekend.

Caitlin would probably do things up right. There was sure to be a barbecue, some music, a lot of old friends coming by…and no wife hanging over his shoulder to spoil things. Not that Natalie had ever done that but there was something to be said about spending a few days just being a good ol' boy, no female company whatsoever. Excluding Caitlin, of course, but Catie never got in the way. She was one of the guys herself, damn near, and always had been.

Gage took a critical look at what he'd packed, took out a pair of trousers and substituted a second pair of jeans. Yessir, this long weekend might be just what he needed, a chance to get away from his problems and relax.

Not that he had any problems. The more time that passed, the more certain he was that Natalie had done them both a favor. If they hadn't had a fight, if she hadn't moved out, who knew how long this sham of a marriage would have dragged on?

"Forever," Gage said, and shut the suitcase.

Forever, because even though he wasn't happy, he wasn't unhappy enough to have done anything about it. He'd just have let things continue as they were, and that would have been a big mistake. He was still young, he had worlds to conquer and things to do. And if Natalie didn't want to share his life, so be it.

There were other women out there. There always had been. A man had to be dead not to notice how many beautiful females smiled a certain way when they met you. He'd long ago stopped being amazed by how often a secretary or a flight attendant would tuck a bit of paper containing a hastily scrawled name and telephone number into his hand, and he knew damn well that many of the women who handed him a business card didn't have anything resembling business on their minds.

Just because he'd never followed up on any of it didn't mean it was too late to start.

Gage carried his suitcase out to his car and tossed it in the back. There might even be some interesting women at Espada this weekend. Not that he'd do anything about it. He'd have to tell his family about his upcoming divorce and he wasn't ready to do that yet, plus it just wouldn't be ethical. Maybe it was old-fashioned, but he wouldn't feel free to date until the lawyers had worked out a formal separation…which reminded him, he really had to get in touch with Grant. Or maybe just somebody local. It wasn't as if he needed an old pal to hold his hand through what lay ahead.

Gage slid behind the wheel of the Vette and stepped on the gas. Yes, as soon as he had a minute, he'd start the ball rolling. Natalie certainly hadn't wasted any time. Jim Rutherford had called yesterday, sounding brisk and efficient, and asked who was representing him. Gage had said he had no time to discuss things right then.

"I'm going out of town," he'd told Rutherford. "Look, you have my assurance that I'll continue to meet my wife's obligations and that I'm willing to assume all her debts until we get this matter settled. I'll have my lawyer contact you when I get back."

Jim had seemed surprised by what he'd said but there was no reason not to be civilized about this thing, considering that he wanted out as much as Natalie did. Oh, it was going to be fine, being a free man again. Amazing, how easily he'd gotten used to the idea.

Gage checked his mirror, then shot onto the highway. Yessir, he'd made a damned fine adjustment.

He hardly thought about Natalie at all. Okay, maybe he hadn't slept any better last night than he had the previous nights, but that was to be expected. His life was changing. All he needed was time to adapt.

Too bad he'd never saved any of those phone numbers he'd been handed but there were plenty of fish in the sea. Just as soon as he had a legal separation, he'd start dating.

Natalie would, too.

Gage frowned.

Once there was a legal separation… She'd wait for that,

wouldn't she? Not that he really cared. It was just that it was the right thing to do.

"Hell," he growled.

He glanced in the mirror, sped across three lanes of traffic, and headed for the exit.

Natalie's apartment was in a section of town that had flip-flopped more times than a politician ducking an issue.

One glance at the building itself was like taking a quick tour through the history of Miami Beach.

It had probably once been elegant, with its Art Deco trim and its marble steps. But the steps were dirty and the trim was chipped, testament to what changing tastes and populations could do to a place. Sometime in the sixties, number 4752 South Egret had become a haven for old folks from the northeast who were looking to live their golden years in the sun. Then the Golden Oldies had given way to Cubans fleeing the politics of their island. The blood-hot beat of salsa had served as counterpoint to the staid waltz time of Lawrence Welk.

Now, the building was caught midway between the past and the future. And the future, Gage thought as he stepped into the vestibule, was anybody's guess.

Someone had done a handsome painting of palm trees and sunshine on the inner door but someone with less artistic sensibility had scrawled a short, ugly word over one of the palms.

The art critic had also punched out the lock.

Gage glanced at the row of names and call bells on the wall. There was no point in bothering with the bells, not when the door swung open at a touch. The name cards were interesting, and read like a veritable United Nations: Romero; Smith; Davidowitz; O'Brien; Dellatorre; Greenberg; Cruz.

And Baron, in Apartment 405. Well, that was something. He'd half expected Natalie to have given up her married name with her marriage.

The stairway ascended through a symphony of smells, the piquant scent of island spices mingling with the less exotic smell of frying chicken. It wasn't unpleasant but it was a long way from the vanilla potpourri Natalie used—had used—around their house.

She'd begun using potpourri a long time ago, in that first little apartment in New York. He still remembered coming home from work one night to find her sitting cross-legged in the middle of their bed because there really hadn't been anyplace else to sit, filling a tiny wicker basket with what looked like dried leaves and twigs.

His brows had raised in question, but when he'd bent down to kiss her and gotten a whiff of the stuff, he'd smiled.

"Mmm," he'd said. "Nice. Who'd have ever figured vanilla could be a turn-on?"

Natalie had laughed and called him silly, which was true enough because the real turn-on was her. And he'd proved it by tumbling her back on the bed, scattering the potpourri so that they made love on a sea of vanilla...

Gage scowled as he reached the last landing.

"So what?" he muttered. This wasn't a walk down memory lane. He'd come here to—to—

To what?

He paused outside Natalie's door, his finger an inch from the bell.

Why had he come here? He should have been in his plane by now, flying over the Gulf instead of standing here, staring at the graffiti-scarred door of his ex-wife's—his almost-ex-wife's—apartment.

Gage leaned closer. He could hear music playing, something with lots of violins and cellos. Chamber music, Natalie called it. The house had always been filled with the sound. Not lately, of course, and it occurred to him that he missed it. He'd have to check the CDs in the den, figure out what it was she used to play, put the disks on...

His scowl deepened. What a ridiculous thought! He'd never liked chamber music, he'd only pretended to. He'd tolerated it for Natalie's sake, which only went to prove what nonsense a man could go through trying to convince himself he still loved his wife, but that was over and done with. Hell, he didn't even know what he was doing, standing around—

The door swung open. Natalie, wearing jeans, a sweatshirt, and a shocked expression, stared at him.

"Gage?"

He frowned, cleared his throat, and tried to figure out what in hell to say.

"What are you doing here, Gage?"

"I, ah, I must have leaned on the doorbell."

"I mean, what are you *doing* here?"

A door creaked open across the hall. Natalie peered past his shoulder, rolled her eyes, and stepped aside.

"Well, don't just stand there," she said impatiently. "Come on in."

He nodded and moved past her, into a narrow hallway.

"Nice," he said automatically.

It wasn't. The light was dim but he could see the cracked linoleum floor and the paint peeling from walls. Natalie shut the door, locked it, and led the way into a living room the size of a grocery carton. He took a quick look around. The walls were painted a sickening dark pink. The carpet, if you could call it that, was stained and frayed. Except for a sagging chair, a beaten-up old table and a small stereo, the room was bare.

Natalie marched to the stereo and hit a button. The music stopped. She turned and faced him, arms folded.

"I don't remember inviting you here."

Gage forced a smile to his lips. "I could say I was in the neighborhood and decided to drop in."

"You could, but I wouldn't believe you."

"Come on, Nat. We may not be living together anymore but we don't have to be enemies, do we?"

It seemed to take forever before she shook her head.

"I guess not. But you should have called first."

"If I had, would you have invited me up?"

Natalie sighed. "No," she admitted, "I wouldn't."

"See?" Gage offered his most charming smile. "That's why I invited myself."

He said it as if it made perfect sense. Well, she thought, maybe it did. It was hard to understand anything right now. Her pulse had leaped at the sight of her husband—her soon-to-be ex—husband—lounging in her doorway, but why wouldn't it? Gage had caught her by surprise. Surely, that was the only reason her heart was racing.

"Come on, Nat. Pour me a cup of coffee. Talk to me. You can't blame me for wanting to know how you're doing."

She considered his request. What harm could come of being polite? Not that she was going to go out of her way to be too gracious.

"Nat?"

Natalie shrugged her shoulders. "I only have instant."

"Instant's fine," he said before she could change her mind.

He tried not to grimace as he followed her into a kitchen that had probably once been white but was faded now to a sad yellow. The cabinets that lined one wall were fashionably doorless though not by design, considering the hinges that still hung from some of them. The stove and refrigerator might have garnered points at an antique show, assuming you were into chipped enamel and uneven legs.

Natalie looked at him. There was a defiant glint in her eyes, as if this were some kind of test.

"Uh, it's...cozy," he said with a quick smile, but he knew, right away, that he'd said the wrong thing.

"Don't patronize me," she said sharply.

"I wasn't—"

"Yes, you were. I know what this place looks like." She turned her back to him, filled a kettle with water and set it on the burner. "This place needs...work."

What it needed was a miracle, but he knew better than to say so. Instead, he kept his silence as Natalie took a jar of coffee from one of the doorless cabinets and a spoon from a drawer that didn't quite close, but he lost it when she reached for a box of safety matches.

"What are you doing? Doesn't that thing have a pilot light?"

"Of course it does. But it doesn't—"

"Dammit!" He snatched the box from her hand. "What are you trying to do? Blow yourself to kingdom come?"

"I am perfectly capable of lighting a stove."

"And it's perfectly capable of blowing up in your face." Gage lit the burner, blew out the match and tossed it into the sink. "Did you tell your landlord this thing needs to be fixed?"

"Sit down, Gage. Do you still take your coffee black?"

Did he still…? She'd only been gone a week. Did she really think he'd have changed his habits in so short a time? Or was he supposed to assume she'd forgotten? The possibility ticked him off.

"Yes," he said curtly. "And answer my question. Does your landlord know about the stove?"

Natalie slapped a mug on the table in front of him. "That's none of your business. This is my apartment, my stove, my life."

"Take it easy, lady. When I ask you a civil question, I'm entitled to a civil answer."

"Ha!"

"Ha? What in hell is *that* supposed to mean?"

"It means," she said coldly, "that you didn't come here to be civil, or to pay a friendly visit."

"The woman's turned into a mind reader," Gage said to the walls.

"You came to criticize. To belittle. To make it clear that my living arrangements don't suit you."

Don't say anything, he told himself. Don't get sidetracked into an argument.

"Well, let me assure you, Mr. Baron. They suit me just fine."

Gage snorted. "Come off it, babe. These 'living arrangements,' as you call them, wouldn't suit a cockroach! This place is—"

"Mine." Natalie's chin lifted. "All mine. And if you don't like it, that's just too bad."

"So much for civility."

"You don't have the right to tell me what to do."

"God, I don't believe this! Are you drawing up a list of grievances for your lawyer?" A muscle knotted in his cheek. "You know damn well I never bossed you around."

A flush rose in Natalie's cheeks. "I was simply reminding you that you're not my husband anymore."

"That's the second time you've made that point," he said softly.

"Well, it's the truth."

Something dark and dangerous flared in his eyes. "Would you like me to prove that you and I are still man and wife, babe?"

Natalie's heart bumped against her ribs as Gage kicked back his chair, rose from the table and came towards her. Her gaze flew over him, taking in the faint stubble on his jaw, the T-shirt that clung to his wide shoulders, the faded, snug jeans. A slow, liquid warmth spread through her blood.

"Don't," she said. "Gage…"

"Don't, what?" He stepped closer, until only a breath separated them. His eyes dropped to her mouth. "You're still my wife, Natalie."

"No. I'm not. I…" She caught her breath as he put his hand against her cheek, stroked back her hair, and curled his fingers around the nape of her neck.

His smile was lazy, sexy, and completely masculine. "If you don't believe me," he said softly, "I'll show you." And he lowered his head and kissed her.

She told herself it was only a kiss, nothing more. A woman could withstand a kiss, even from a man like Gage…

But when he cupped her face in his hands, brushed his lips against her, then took her mouth again, she was lost.

"Gage," she whispered, and opened her mouth to his.

With a groan, he gathered her into his arms and kissed her hungrily. Her hands rose, pressed against his chest. She could feel the gallop of his heart, feel the heat of his flesh through his thin cotton shirt. She turned her face into his neck, inhaling his familiar scent, tasting the saltiness of his skin. Her hand dropped to his waist, then lower, and he groaned again.

Oh, how she had missed him. Gage. Her husband. The only man she'd ever loved.

Gage shut his eyes as Natalie bit lightly at his throat. God, how he'd missed her. His wife. The only woman he'd ever loved.

This was right. So right. Holding her, kissing her, inhaling her wildflower scent and, now, the intoxicating scent of her passion.

He whispered her name as he cupped her bottom, lifted her into him, moved against her so she could feel the urgency of his need. She had to remember how it used to be between them, how it could be again...

A wild shriek pierced the silence. Natalie jumped like a startled rabbit. Her eyes flew open.

Gage muttered an oath. "It's just the kettle." He reached back, fumbled for the control knob on the stove. "Easy, babe. It's okay—"

"It isn't." Natalie slammed her hands against his chest and pushed free of his embrace. "Is that why you came here?" Her voice trembled with anger; her cheeks were bright pink. "To seduce me?"

Was that what she thought had just happened between them? Seduction? Gage's eyes narrowed.

"I thought we were making love."

She'd thought so, too...but admitting that, to him or to herself, would be crazy.

"It was sex," she said. "That's all it was. Sex. And it was a mistake. Am I making myself clear?"

His mouth thinned. She certainly was. Sex was all the last few minutes had been for her. His wife—his once-upon-a-time wife—had turned into a stranger. And he didn't much like the stranger she'd become.

"Perfectly clear," he said. "But you've got it wrong, babe.

I wouldn't try to seduce you if you turned up at my door naked, gift-wrapped and with a bow around your neck.''

The color drained from Natalie's face. "Get out."

"Trust me." Gage strode from the kitchen. "I'm going."

"Good." Natalie elbowed past him. "And," she said as she yanked the door open, "don't bother coming—"

"Natalie?"

Gage swung towards the door, and the man standing in it. Man, hell. A mountain was more like it. A giant, with flowing blond hair, a neck the size of a tree trunk, with biceps and thighs to match. And, from the look of rage on the giant's face, Gage figured the guy was about to turn him into mince-meat.

"Hans," Natalie said. "What are you doing here?"

"I was just unlocking my door." The giant jerked his head towards the apartment across the hall, though his eyes never left Gage's face. "And I heard voices." His hands knotted at his sides. "Is this punk giving you trouble, Natalie?"

"No. No, Hans, you don't understand..."

"I'm not a punk," Gage said with a feral smile. "I'm her husband."

"Ex-husband." Hans's eyes narrowed. "Natalie is divorced."

"Separated," Natalie said quickly.

"Neither," Gage said just as quickly. "Anyway, what's it to you?"

The giant took a step forward. "Natalie is my friend. If she needs help, I am here to offer it."

"Hans. Really. I don't—"

"That's right, Hans." Gage smiled. He could feel his adrenaline pumping. So what if the guy outweighed him by a ton? So what if he looked like King Kong on steroids? Gage felt pumped enough to take him. And hell, if he couldn't, that was okay, too. A couple of rounds with Hans the Watchdog sounded like fun right about now.

Gage took a step forward. "You heard the lady. She

doesn't need you. Not for anything. You got that, or do you want me to spell it out?''

"Stop it!" Natalie pushed between the two men and looked from one angry face to the other. "This is ridiculous."

Hans folded his massive arms against his chest. "You say the word, Natalie, and I will throw him out."

"Yeah, babe." Gage grinned, bounced lightly on his toes. "Say the word and I'll put old Hans into his apartment without bothering to open the door."

Natalie put a hand on each man's chest. "Hans," she said firmly, "go home. My ex—"

"Her husband," Gage said, the maniacal smile still plastered to his face.

"The man I no longer live with," Natalie said coldly, "is an idiot, but he's harmless."

"You are positive?"

"Yes."

"Okay." Hans puffed out his breath. "But if you need me..."

"I'll call you."

"Good. And Natalie... That movie we talked about is on later. If you want to watch it with me—"

"Great." Natalie smiled brightly. "I'll make some popcorn."

The giant flashed one last look at Gage. Gage gave him a smile that showed all his teeth.

"*Auf weidersein,* pal," he said, and slammed the door in his face.

"Your humor was wasted," Natalie snapped. "Hans is Dutch."

"I don't care if he's Martian. Movies? Popcorn? In case you've forgotten, babe, you're still a married woman."

"Only temporarily. Besides, Hans is just a friend."

"A friend, huh?"

"I know the concept of a man and woman having a relationship based on anything but sex is impossible for you to imagine, but it happens."

"That guy has only one thing on his mind. He wants to get into your pants."

"You are so crude!"

"I'm honest."

"Well, you're wrong. Besides, it's none of your—"

"But it is." Gage's jaw shot forward. Enough was enough. Whether she liked it or not, he was still her husband. And it was time she knew it.

"Get your things," he growled.

"Give it up, Gage. I'm not taking orders from you."

"Pack enough for the weekend. And make it quick."

"Oh, I just love this," Natalie said pleasantly. "Am I supposed to click my heels? Because if I am—"

"It's my father," Gage said, lying easily, mercilessly, and creatively through his clenched teeth.

The smirk fell from Natalie's face. "Jonas?"

Gage nodded. "That's what I came here to tell you." Well, it wasn't a lie. Something had happened. After all, a man didn't turn eighty-five every day. "I've spoken with my brothers. We're all flying to Espada."

"Oh." Natalie bit her bottom lip. "I'm so sorry. But—"

"I figured you'd be willing to set our personal problems aside, go with me, so that the old man can see you one more time."

Well, that wasn't a lie, either. One more time than Jonas had already seen her was one more time, wasn't it? Besides, there wasn't a way in hell he was going to leave Natalie here. Not in this hellhole. Not with Hans across the hall.

"Why didn't you tell me this right away?"

Gage met his wife's suspicious look with a bland smile.

"We got sidetracked, babe. Remember?"

She blushed, but only a little. "Gage, I swear, if you're lying to me…"

"Cross my heart," he said, wide-eyed.

Natalie folded her arms, rocked back on her heels and looked at him. He'd almost given up hope when she puffed out her breath.

"Okay. Give me a few minutes to pack."

It was hard not to grin but Gage controlled himself until Natalie had left the room. Then he mouthed a silent "yes" and pumped his fist into the air.

CHAPTER FIVE

NATALIE disappeared into her bedroom and emerged ten minutes later carrying a small suitcase. She'd changed from paint-smeared jeans and a T-shirt to a somber linen suit.

"I'm ready," she said.

Gage nodded and took the overnight case from her. The suit, he suspected, offered a clue as to what she'd packed. Sickroom stuff. Hospital stuff. Maybe even funeral parlor stuff.

She was going to be furious when she realized she'd been had.

Maybe he ought to tell her the truth. Maybe he ought to give her the option of going to this party or of staying behind. Maybe...

But there was no "maybe" here. A woman in the process of divorce wasn't about to say, certainly, she'd love to go away with her almost-ex for the weekend. Given a choice, Natalie would stay right where she was, with entertainment provided courtesy of Hans and a bowl of popcorn.

"Gage? Are we going or aren't we?"

The decision was a no-brainer. "Of course we're going," he said.

How much of a fuss could Natalie make once they reached Espada?

He kept waiting for the questions to start on the way to the airport.

What, exactly, was wrong with Jonas? Had he been hospitalized? What did the doctors say? How much time did they have?

He waited, but Natalie didn't say a word. Not one single, solitary word.

Either she was angry about how he'd behaved in that hovel she called an apartment or she figured that the protocol for people on the brink of divorce was silence.

Gage didn't care. He was just glad she wasn't pressing him for details about his father's imminent demise because he sure as hell didn't have any.

The Cessna was ready and waiting. Natalie climbed in, put on her headset and fastened her seat belt, then froze him with a look when he reached over to check the belt, the way he'd done a thousand times before.

"I am perfectly capable of buckling my belt," she said coldly.

Uh-huh. Okay. So, it was going to be that kind of a flight, was it? And it was only going to get worse once they reached Espada and she realized he'd lied to her.

No. Not lied. He'd, uh, he'd just left out a few pertinent details. And for a very good reason.

Gage's jaw tightened as he taxied the plane onto the runway.

What sort of man would leave a woman in a hellhole like that apartment? What sort would leave her to the tender mercies of Hans, who was coming on to her with all the delicacy of a waltzing hippopotamus? Not one who understood his responsibilities, that was certain. Natalie would probably never understand that, but she didn't have to. It was enough that he understood, and that he'd taken action.

But, man, all hell was going to break loose when they reached the ranch and she found out that the only thing wrong with Jonas was that he was still the same opinionated, intransigent old bastard he'd always been. And there wasn't a darned thing new about that.

"Gage?"

Natalie's voice sounded clearly over the microphone.

"Yes?"

"What's wrong with Jonas?"

Okay, he thought, here we go.

"I'm not sure."

"Haven't the doctors been able to diagnose it yet?"

"No. No, they haven't."

"Did he collapse? Have some kind of attack? Surely, they must suspect something."

"Nothing, as far as I know." Well, that was the truth. The doctors *didn't* suspect anything because there was nothing to suspect, unless terminal pigheadedness could be classified as a disease.

"He's never been sick a day in his life."

"Yes, but Jonas is an old man." If he stuck to the facts, the truth couldn't hurt him. He was definitely thinking on his feet.

"Who called to tell you he was ill? Abel? Marta? Leighton?"

Gage frowned. "Hand me that chart, would you? No, not that one. Yeah, that's it. Thanks."

He spread the chart in his lap. How long could he pretend to be studying their route? A minute? Two? Long enough to figure out an answer that wouldn't give the game away, although any answer was probably going to be a bad one. It didn't really matter if the call had come from Espada's manager, from Jonas's wife or from his nephew. Any of those people would be expected to have provided details Gage certainly didn't have.

"Gage? Did you hear me?"

He folded the chart, tucked it away and glanced at his wife as the plane gained altitude.

Maybe now was the time to tell her. They were a mile in the air. What could she do when she found out he'd stretched the truth?

Anything, ranging from slugging him silly to demanding he take her back to Miami. He just didn't know, and that was the problem. He didn't know his wife anymore. Where was the sweet girl he'd married? The girl who'd loved him enough to run away with him? What had become of the helpmate who'd seen him through grad school? Who'd urged him to transfer out of law school after he'd realized he'd have made a lousy lawyer? Where had she gone, the girl who'd worked night and day at his side helping him build Baron Resorts?

She was gone, vanquished by the steely-eyed female who sat beside him now.

Maybe he'd made a mistake, setting things up so Natalie would come with him to Espada. Her life was her own; her choices no longer involved him.

He could turn the plane around, then say to her, "Natalie, Jonas is fine. There's no reason for you to come with me. Actually, Nat, we both know that you don't want to be with me. And that's okay because I don't want to be with you. If you prefer to spend the evening with that bozo, Hans, that's your affair. Hell, if you want to spend the night with..."

"Gage, I want some answers. What's wrong with Jonas?"

He looked at her. "Sorry?"

"I said—"

"There must be something wrong with your microphone. All I'm getting is static."

"Can't you hear me?"

"No good." He tapped his headset. "You're not coming through."

Natalie frowned, adjusted her mike and spoke louder. "I said..."

"Nothing but static," he shouted, trying not to wince because her raised voice felt as if it had nearly punctured his eardrums. "I can't hear a thing you're saying."

She gave him a long, hard look. "You'd better not be lying about Jonas, Gage Baron, or so help me Hannah, I'm going to kill you."

Gage's smile was all innocence. "Sorry. I can't make out a word."

Natalie frowned. Then she settled back in her seat, folded her arms, and stared straight out the window.

By the time they were over the Gulf, Natalie was fuming.

Why hadn't she thought of questioning Gage before she'd climbed into the plane?

Jonas was dying? Somehow, it didn't seem possible. Jonas was too mean to die. Besides, if that was why Gage had come by her apartment, wouldn't he have said something about his father's illness right away, instead of first doing everything he possibly could, short of pawing the ground, to make Hans think he still had some claim to her?

And he didn't. He most certainly didn't, and the sooner he got that through his thick skull, the better.

There was something fishy about this situation, she was sure of it. There wasn't a thing wrong with Jonas. Not a thing. She could feel it in her bones.

She was flying to Texas with her soon-to-be ex-husband for no reason whatsoever, except that Gage had taken one look at her and her new life and decided that he just couldn't tolerate the fact that she could *have* a life without him.

She wondered what he'd say if she turned and told him that; if she said, "Yes, I can, indeed, live without you. I found my own apartment, I've already interviewed for a couple of jobs, I've even managed to make friends. I don't need you anymore, Gage Baron..."

But how could she say that, when it would be a lie?

She did need him, she must, or else why would she awaken each morning with that terrible emptiness in her heart? With tears on her cheeks and Gage's name on her lips?

Natalie shifted in her seat.

Habit, that was the reason. Of course it was. Once Liz Holcomb had gotten past the shock of Natalie's announcement, they'd had a long, long talk. And one of the things Liz had talked about was how weird it had felt when she'd divorced her first husband.

"It's like giving up smoking," she'd said. "You know what I mean? You realize it's a good thing you've done but the habit dies hard."

Precisely.

You didn't live with a man for ten years and then grow accustomed to living without him in the blink of an eye. Habit, that was all that empty feeling was. And even bad habits were tough to break.

She was adjusting, though, little by little. Already, she could see how many good things there were to consider about her new life.

Little things, some of them. Like not finding the toilet seat up when it should have been down. Like no wet bath towels draped over the shower door. And if she wanted to read in the middle of the night there was nobody lying beside her to groan, roll onto his belly, put his pillow over his head and say, in that martyred voice, "No, that's fine, the light doesn't bother me at all."

Even better, there was nobody to sit and wait aimlessly for at the end of the day, though why she had, the past couple of years, was beyond her comprehension. Why wait for a man who'd almost invariably phone at seven o'clock to tell you he wouldn't be home for dinner, when you'd already figured that out an hour ago? Why even be there when he finally breezed in at nine or ten or later, aimed a kiss in your direction and said, "Hello, I'm exhausted, good night, I'll see you in the morning, and oh, by the way, how was your day..." all in one breath? If he came home at all. If he didn't spend the night, a week's worth of nights, in California or Vermont or Bali or any damned place on the planet except his own bed, with his own wife.

The gall of him, expecting her to turn into a hot-blooded sex kitten the times he *was* in that bed. There was more to living together than sex but Gage seemed to have forgotten that.

Tears burned in Natalie's eyes. Angry tears. She certainly didn't feel anything for him anymore. Nothing but anger, at the way he'd eliminated her from his existence, except when he wanted physical relief or when he needed her to look like the elegantly gowned-and-groomed trophy she had become.

No, she didn't feel anything for him. And that was fine. She didn't want to feel anything for him, not anymore. Not ever. Not—

The Cessna banked to the right.

"Espada," Gage said, and jerked his head towards her window.

Natalie looked, but tears blurred her vision. She didn't have to see what was out there; she knew every inch of this place. The dusty airstrip, the endless acres of brown earth, the rolling green hills, the butte where she and Gage had first made love.

Espada, where their life together had begun. Now they were returning to it, when everything between them was over.

She'd left this place ten years ago, run away with Gage because they'd been too much in love to let anyone or anything keep them apart. And she still loved him, heaven help her, loved this man who'd turned into someone she didn't know and didn't even like.

She couldn't spend the weekend with him here. It would be too painful. If Jonas was on his deathbed, she'd pay her respects, then ask Abel or one of the ranch hands to drive her to the airport in Austin.

If Jonas was on his deathbed, she thought, and at that moment she knew, absolutely knew, that he wasn't.

She swung towards Gage as the plane's wheels touched down.

"It's not true, is it?"

"What?" Gage motioned to his headset. "I can't—"

"Oh, stop it! Don't make it worse by lying some more!" Natalie slammed her fist into his shoulder. "Admit it!"

"Dammit, Nat, are you nuts? Stop bouncing around. And stop slugging me. You want us to crash?"

"Crash into what? We're on the ground and there's miles and miles of—of nothing out there." She punched him again as he shut off the engines. "You lied about not being able to hear me. And about Jonas."

"Now, Natalie—"

"Don't you 'now, Natalie' me, Gage Baron. If you think that—that kidnapping me is going to stop me from..."

"Just listen to yourself," Gage said. "I'm a liar. A kidnapper. What's next? Am I a serial killer, too, just because we haven't been able to work out our little problem?"

"You call a divorce 'little'?"

"Considering the reason we're here, I do."

"What reason?" Natalie glared at him. "Or are you going to go on pretending your father's at death's door?"

Gage cleared his throat. "I, ah, I never said—"

Natalie flung her door open. "He'd better be," she snapped. "You hear me, Gage? Jonas had damn well better be dying, or—"

"Or what?" a leathery voice demanded.

Natalie looked around. Her father-in-law was standing beside the wing, looking as indestructible as ever. He was smiling, too, as if to remind her that, over the years, he'd accepted his son's decision to marry beneath him.

"Jonas." Natalie flushed. "I didn't mean—"

"I hope not, because unless you know somethin' I don't, I'm a long way from breathing my last." Jonas Baron held out his arms. "Let me help you down and then you can tell me why you're determined to hurry me into my grave."

She didn't tell him.

How could she say, "Jonas, your son brought me here under false pretences because he doesn't like the idea that I've left him"? when standing right behind her father-in-law were Travis and Slade and Caitlin. The entire Baron clan was waiting to greet her with hugs and kisses. It was not really the right moment to point out that she wasn't supposed to be there because she and one of the clan members were getting a divorce.

So Natalie smiled brightly and lied every bit as glibly as her husband. Jonas, she said, had misunderstood her. She hadn't said "dying," she'd said "trying"; that what she'd meant was that Gage had told her Jonas was *trying* to get them all gathered together for the weekend, and the more she talked the worse it sounded and the more puzzled her in-laws's faces became until, finally, Gage jumped into the conversation and said he'd been away and he'd phoned home and left a message on the machine for Natalie but the machine must have garbled it.

Jonas frowned and said that didn't make any sense.

"You got your invitation by courier, boy, ten days ago, same as your brothers."

"Yeah," Travis said, "remember? Slade and I called you and you said—"

"Oh, for God's sake," Caitlin said briskly, "who gives a damn what anybody said? Nat, you come on in the truck with me. Let the men talk themselves to death in the Jeep."

Natalie threw her a grateful smile. "Bless you, Catie," she whispered as Caitlin put an arm around her waist and hurried her off.

"Bless me, my foot," Caitlin whispered back, peering at Natalie from under a cluster of escaped auburn curls. "What in the Sam Hill is going on with you and that dumb brother of mine?"

Natalie's smile lit the cab of the truck as Caitlin got behind the steering wheel. "Not a thing," she said, and burst into tears.

Gage figured that things were so bad that the day couldn't get any worse.

His brothers had given him funny looks when Natalie launched into that tongue twister of an explanation after getting off the plane, but Caitlin had rushed her away so quickly that there'd been no time for questions.

And then Jonas had ordered his sons into the Jeep and they'd set off for the house in a bone-jarring ride that had raised enough dust to cover all the Barons from head to toe. Now they were sitting in the library, every one of them except the old man trying his best not to spread that dust over the leather chairs and mahogany furniture.

There was a tap at the door.

"What?" Jonas roared.

Marta Baron, wife number five, poked her head into the room.

"I just wanted to say hello to Gage, and see if you gentlemen wanted anything."

Gage got to his feet and crossed the room. Marta was sixtyish, elegant, and—as far as he could tell—the best of the old man's wives. That she'd lasted more than a year still amazed him.

"Hello, gorgeous," he said, kissing her cheek. "Still hanging in there, I see."

Marta smiled. "I'm here for the duration."

"Babble, babble, babble," Jonas said irritably. "You can play catch-up at lunch, Marta. Right now, my sons and I have things to discuss."

"Certainly," Marta said pleasantly. She patted Gage's cheek, winked at Slade and Travis, and the door swung shut.

Jonas sank back into his chair, stretched out his legs and crossed his scuffed boots at the ankles.

"Well, this certainly is an occasion. All my sons, under one roof." He smiled thinly. "All it takes, apparently, is thinkin' that I'm at death's door."

Gage cleared his throat. "Natalie didn't mean—"

"I'm not talkin' about Natalie. You're here, and your brothers are here. And a bunch of butt-kissers are comin' by for the weekend. Am I really supposed to think that would have happened if I weren't approachin' my eighty-fifth birthday?"

Travis sighed. "Just because you're going to be eighty-five doesn't mean—"

"Bull patties. If I'm not at death's door, I'm certainly in its anteroom. Can we at least agree on that?"

"What's agreed," Slade said pleasantly, "is that we've come here to celebrate your birthday, not to quarrel with you."

Jonas looked at all three of them. Then he turned away, picked up a wooden box and flipped it open to expose a row of Cuban cigars.

"Have one," he said. Gage, Travis, and Slade all politely declined. The old man snorted, plucked a cigar from the box, bit off the tip and spat it into a heavy crystal ashtray. "Figured you boys would have grown up enough to appreciate a fine cigar by now."

His sons made no response. Jonas sighed, lit up and puffed out a cloud of smoke. "Nothing like a fine cigar," he said, "except maybe a fine woman."

Gage flashed a look at Slade, who rolled his eyes. Or a shot of good bourbon, Slade mouthed silently...

"Or a shot of good bourbon," Jonas said. He rose, walked

to the mahogany sideboard, took four crystal glasses from a shelf, then opened a bottle of Jack Daniel's. "Are you boys grown up enough for that?"

"Yes," Travis said, and smiled. "But I suspect you know that Gage would rather have an ale, Slade would prefer a beer, and I'd opt for a glass of whatever red wine is open."

Jonas chuckled. "Some things just don't change."

"No," Gage said, "they don't."

The old man's bushy white eyebrows lifted. "Testy mood you're in, boy. That wife of yours givin' you a hard time?"

Gage looked at his father. "No," he said coldly.

"'Course she is. The temperature in that airplane couldn't have been a degree above freezin'."

"You're wrong, Father."

Jonas contemplated the tip of his cigar. "I'm never wrong."

"You like to think so."

"I know so. Didn't I try to tell you that girl would only bring you misery?"

"You did tell me. A thousand times, at least. But you were wrong. And I'd appreciate it if you'd remember that that 'girl' is a woman, and her name is Natalie."

"I know her name," Jonas said mildly.

"Then please use it."

"Gage." Travis's voice was quiet, but it had a warning edge. "Father...let's calm down, okay? Slade's right. We're here to celebrate your birthday. Surely we can get through the weekend without quarreling."

"And I didn't invite you here for that purpose," Jonas said brusquely. He held the bottle of bourbon over the glasses. "Yes or no? You boys prefer your piss-water, you can have it. Got it all right over there, at the bar."

Gage sighed. It was a challenge. He knew it, and he knew his brothers knew it. Travis and Slade were right. It was the old man's birthday weekend.

"Sure," he said, and forced the image of a cold ale from his mind, "why not?"

Travis and Slade looked as if they'd cheerfully throttle him, given the chance, but they nodded in agreement.

Jonas poured, tipped a drop of water into each glass, then raised his in a toast.

"To the Baron dynasty. And to my sons, who are its future."

Gage, Slade and Travis paused with their glasses halfway to their mouths, stopped cold by the untypical sentiment. They looked at each other, then at their father.

"You *are* ill," Travis said flatly.

Jonas snorted. "I'm as fit as a bull in season, boy."

"Well, in that case... Thank you, Father. I'm sure Gage and Slade are as pleased as I am that you feel—"

"'Course, I'm not fool enough to think all three of you see it that way."

Gage looked at his brothers, who shrugged. "Sorry?"

"Sorry for what, boy?" Jonas puffed out a cloud of cigar smoke. "Far as I can tell, you haven't done anythin' to apologize for. Not yet, anyway."

"I meant that I didn't understand what you just said, Father. About us being your future but not seeing it that way."

"I didn't say you boys were my future. I said you were *the* future. A man works his ass off all his life, he don't want to see it all go to the grave with him."

Slade stretched out his legs and crossed his booted feet. "You're a long way from the grave, Pop," he said lazily.

"Sit up straight. Don't call me 'Pop.' Don't tell me lies, neither. I'm eighty-five tomorrow. How much longer do you think I've got?" Jonas tossed back the last of his bourbon, put down his glass and ground his cigar into it. "Here's the situation. Baron Oil and Baron Mining, Baron Properties...every last one of my companies can go on without me. You know that, or you should, considerin' that you three sit on their boards."

"Dollar-a-year men, Father," Gage said with a glittering smile. "We don't take a penny from you. And we'd appreciate it if you'd remember that."

Jonas laughed. "Standin' up to me, are you, boy? Well, that's fine. You might not have learned how to smoke a cigar or to handle that wife of yours—"

Gage shot to his feet. "Are we back to that crap?"

"Gage," Slade said softly, "take it easy."

"No. Hell, no. I want to know what that remark means."

"Don't bust a gut, boy. Any fool could tell that girl— pardon me—could tell that your Natalie would sooner have found herself standing next to a rattler than next to you."

Gage glared at his father. "Maybe she finally figured out that your blood flows in my veins," he said, and walked out of the room.

Slade and Travis found him exactly where they'd expected to find him, sitting on a bale of hay up in the loft of the old barn where they used to gather when they were boys and called themselves Los Lobos.

"By God," Slade said as he sank down beside Gage, "I can't believe we really used to hang out in this place."

Travis grinned as he settled opposite them. "Hey, Brother Wolves, we were kids, and kids aren't noted for being too clever."

"Seems as though I haven't made much progress from then to now," Gage said glumly. He leaned back on his elbows. "Tell me I didn't let the old man get under my skin just now."

Slade sighed. "You want to tell him that, Trav?"

"No way. If one of us is gonna lie, Slade, I figure it might as well be you."

"Okay, okay, I get the message." Gage sat up, plucked a strand of hay from the floor and twirled it between his fingers. "I was an idiot, right?"

"Right," his brothers said in unison.

Gage glowered at them both. "Thanks."

"You're welcome," Slade said, and smiled.

After a moment, Gage smiled, too. "Amazing. I'm thirty-one years old, and he still knows how to push all the right buttons."

"Well," Travis drawled, "of course he does, otherwise he wouldn't be Jonas Baron, now, would he?"

The brothers laughed. There was a silence, and then Travis cleared his throat.

"You want to talk about it?"

Gage shook his head. "No."

"You sure?"

"Positive."

Slade and Travis looked at each other. "Well," Slade said, "in that case—"

"She left me."

"She what?"

"I said, she left me."

"Natalie left you?"

"What is this, a Greek chorus?" Gage glowered at his brothers. "Take a number, okay? One of you speak at a time."

Travis cleared his throat. "Natalie and you split up?"

"No."

"But you just said—"

"He said she left him," Slade said.

"Well, I know he did. But if she left him, that means—"

"Holy Toledo!" Gage jumped to his feet and planted his hands on his hips. "I am right here. Right here, in front of you. You want to talk about me, at least wait until I leave." He stalked towards the ladder that led down from the loft. "Matter of fact, I'll take off right now and give you guys the chance to talk yourselves blue in the face."

"I'm sorry," Travis said quickly.

"Yeah," Slade added. "I'm sorry, too. Come on, Gage, sit down."

Gage took a deep breath. Then he turned and looked at the two of them.

"Hell," he said miserably, "I didn't meant to jump all over you guys. It's just that—that—"

He sank down on the bale of hay again, propped his elbows on his knees and put his face in his hands. Travis and Slade exchanged glances, and then Slade spoke.

"What happened?" he said softly.

Gage sighed, sat up straight and shook his head. "I don't know."

Slade looked at Travis. "He doesn't know."

Travis nodded. "Yeah." He leaned forward and laid a hand on Gage's knee. "It's rough man. I've been there."

"Give me a break, Trav. You were married for, what, a year? Nat and I have been together ten years. Longer, if you count the times we used to sneak around here, avoiding her old man and ours. And Cathy didn't leave you, you left her. For damn good reasons."

"Details," Travis said.

A smile eased across Gage's mouth. "Maybe. But important details, you have to admit."

Travis sat back. "Sure, but it's the same point. I left, but I didn't really know all the reasons I'd left until I'd had time to calm down."

"Look," Gage said tightly, "I'm telling you it isn't the same. Nobody married anybody for money. Nobody cheated on anybody. Nobody's fallen out of love."

"Then, how come Nat left you?" Slade asked.

Gage swung towards him. "How in hell should I know? Dammit, Slade..." His angry words drifted to silence. "She didn't marry me for my money," he said after a minute.

"What money?" Slade said, and Gage laughed.

"Exactly. I had fifty bucks in my pocket the night we ran off to Vegas." He sighed, rose to his feet, tucked his hands into the pockets of his jeans and rocked back on his heels. "And she hasn't cheated on me—and don't either of you risk a fat lip by asking me if I'm sure about that." Gage shrugged his shoulders. "I know Natalie, at least, I used to know her. And no matter what else has changed, that hasn't. She wouldn't do something like that, and you guys know it."

Slade and Travis nodded. "You're right," Travis said. He blew out his breath. "So, that leaves the last thing."

"What thing?"

"The bit about nobody falling out of love."

"Well, nobody has. Dammit all, I've spent the past couple

of weeks trying to convince myself that I don't love Natalie anymore but who am I kidding? I love her. I always have, and I always will."

Slade and Travis exchanged glances and then Slade cleared his throat.

"Yeah," he said carefully, "but that doesn't mean *nobody's* fallen out of love."

"I just told you. Nobody has. I still love..." Gage fell silent. His eyes met his brother's. "Oh, man," he whispered, and shoved both hands through his hair. "She can't have stopped loving me. She can't."

"Well," Travis said after a couple of minutes of endless silence, "you know that old cliché, right? It takes two."

Gage shot him a look that was part fury and part despair.

"Look," Travis said, "I'm not going to lie to you, man. I'm a lawyer. I don't specialize in divorce law but I see enough of it to know that, well, things change."

"No," Slade said firmly. "You're saying that because you've been burned yourself, but what Gage and Nat have is different. Don't give me that look, Travis. I'm right and you know it." He sighed. "Their marriage is the only one I've ever seen that works."

"It did work," Gage said. "And, by God, I'll make it work again. I just need to figure out what went wrong."

"Gage," Travis said gently, "any man who thinks he can get into a woman's head is a man with a big problem. Women are beautiful. They're bright. They're exciting." He shook his head. "But even the good ones, like Natalie, are too complex for any poor bastard in pants to figure out."

"Amen to that," a male voice said.

The brothers swung towards the ladder, and towards the head and shoulders that had appeared.

"Sorry," Slade said politely, "but this is a private—"

Gage rose slowly to his feet. "Grant?" he said in disbelief.

Grant Landon, dressed in a dark suit, starched white shirt and red silk tie, smiled.

"Yeah," he said, batting unsuccessfully at the hay caught in his hair. "It's me." He glanced around the loft, at the all-male contingent, and smiled again. "So, what's the deal here, Gage? Do you have to be a Baron to join this I Don't Understand the Female of the Species Club, or can any poor, benighted S.O.B. become a member?"

Gage, Travis, and Slade grinned.

"You've got the agenda right," Gage said, "but the name of the club is Los Lobos." He looked at his brothers. "Fellow Wolves, what do you think? I can vouch for this guy. He's lean, he's mean…"

"'He's part of the team,'" Slade said, and extended his hand to Grant. "You're in, pal."

"Yeah." Travis shook Grant's hand, too, then smiled as Grant climbed the last rungs of the ladder and stepped into the loft. He eyed him up and down and his smile turned into a grin. "Except, you're gonna have to learn to wear the Los Lobos uniform. Suits, ties and wingtips just don't cut it."

Grant rolled his eyes. "Maybe I joined the wrong club," he said. "You're starting to sound just like my wife."

Gage laughed. Really laughed, which was something he hadn't done in a very long time. Slade and Travis, then Grant Landon, joined in.

And it occurred to Gage that maybe coming home hadn't been such a bad idea, after all.

CHAPTER SIX

CAITLIN McCORD felt helpless.

It was a new and altogether unpleasant sensation, but try as she might, she couldn't feel any other way.

What did you do, when your stepsister-in-law bawled her eyes out? Well, you asked what was wrong. And when she shook her head and went right on crying, you hustled her into the house, up the steps and into her room. Then you asked the question again, and when she blew her nose into a handful of tissues, then looked at you through tear-filled eyes and said that nothing was wrong, that she was weeping and snuffling because of an allergy, you were really at a loss.

Caitlin, naturally, didn't believe any of it. Allergies didn't put that look of despair on a woman's face. Still, if that was the story Natalie wanted her to swallow, she'd pretend to gag it down, at least until she could get Gage alone and find out what he'd done to make his wife so miserable.

Men, after all, were the cause of misery. And Gage, though she loved him dearly, was a man.

So Caitlin smiled and said, oh yes, allergies were horrible things, weren't they? And then, to keep the ball rolling, she'd launched into some light anecdotes about the problems she'd had planning Jonas's big birthday party...

"Birthday party?" Natalie said, looking startled.

"Yes. Well, I suppose you're right. You can't call a weekend celebration something as simple as a party, but—"

"Birthday party," Natalie repeated, and her eyes flashed with anger. "*That's* what's happening to Jonas this weekend? He's celebrating his birthday?"

"Yes," Caitlin said uneasily. Didn't Natalie know? "His eighty-fifth."

"Oh, that rat," Natalie muttered as she sank down on the edge of the bed. "That no-good, rotten, stinking—"

Caitlin sat down beside her. "Some might say that describes my stepfather to a tee, but I take it we're not talking about him," she said with a hesitant smile.

"Gage," Natalie muttered. "Gage, that selfish, arrogant, miserable—"

"He didn't tell you you were coming to Espada for Jonas's birthday party?"

"No," Natalie said calmly, while she plotted ways to murder her soon-to-be ex. "No, he most certainly didn't."

"Oh," Caitlin said, and shut her mouth. One look at Natalie told her that saying anything more would have been like trying to tap dance through a minefield.

"Oh, indeed," Natalie said grimly. She honked one last time into the tissues, then shot to her feet and marched to the mirror. A woman wearing a creased linen suit and a nose as red as Bozo the Clown's glared back at her. "I don't suppose this is going to be a quiet family dinner?"

Caitlin cleared her throat. "You might say that."

Natalie swung around. "Might I also say I won't be able to get away with looking like I picked my outfit up at a rummage sale?"

"It's not a problem," Caitlin said quickly. "You know how my usual tastes run to jeans, boots and sweatshirts. Well, Jonas must have figured I'd turn up like that tonight so he had Neiman Marcus send boxes and boxes of dresses and stuff, and I'd just bet you and I are about the same—"

"Tell me all of it." Natalie folded her arms. "I want to be able to tell Gage exactly why I'm going to kill him."

Caitlin sighed, crossed her booted ankles, folded her hands and looked down into her lap. "It's black tie. Cocktails at seven-thirty, dinner at nine, dancing on the terrace, fireworks at midnight..."

"Fireworks sooner than that," Natalie said coldly. "Who's on the guest list?"

Oh, Gage, Caitlin thought, you are a dead man! "Well, there's the governor and his wife."

"The governor," Natalie said calmly, smoothing down the skirt of her crushed suit. "Go on."

"A couple of U.S. senators. That new Hollywood hunk. Some TV people…"

"And not a one of 'em here for a death watch."

"Huh?"

Natalie slapped her hands on her hips. "I know he's your stepbrother and you love him, but I think it's time you knew that Gage Baron is a genuine, gold-plated stinker."

"Nat, look—"

"Do you know what he did, that brother of yours?"

"Well, I—"

"He showed up at my door," Natalie said, storming across the room, grabbing the carry-on bag she'd packed with nothing more than a change of underwear, a toothbrush and a comb, "showed up uninvited, unannounced—"

"At your door? Natalie, you're losing me here. Isn't your door and his door the same?"

"Not anymore," Natalie snapped—and saw, too late, the look of shock that transformed Caitlin's face. "Oh, Catie," she said, hurrying to her side. "Catie, I'm sorry. I wasn't going to tell you…"

"You and Gage split up?"

Natalie sank down on the edge of the bed. "Yes."

"But—but that can't be." Caitlin clasped Natalie's hands. "You and Gage have the perfect marriage. Not like my mother and her ex's, or Jonas and his."

"I don't know what to tell you, Catie, except that—that things happen. People change."

"But you and Gage…?"

"Me," Natalie said. "And Gage." She pulled her hands free of Catie's and shot to her feet again. "And if he really thinks he can get me to go back to him by—by kidnapping me for the weekend…"

"Is that what he thinks?"

"Apparently."

"He still loves you, then?"

"Love," Natalie said with disdain. "He just doesn't like to lose."

"He wants you back, Nat. Is that right?"

"Look, what's the difference? I'm not going back. I don't want to. I don't love—I don't love..." Natalie's voice broke. "Oh, hell," she said, snatching at the tissues and wiping her eyes. After a minute, she looked at Caitlin. "Obviously, Gage and I can't spend the night together in this room."

"Obviously," Caitlin said calmly.

"You'll have to put me in a different room, Catie."

"Oh, of course." Caitlin mentally crossed her fingers. "And I would, if I could. But there's no space."

"No space? In this huge house?"

"Not even a spare corner."

Well, it wasn't a lie. The guest rooms were all assigned, it was true. The overflow crowd would be staying at a hotel in Austin, shuttled back and forth by a mini fleet of vehicles hired for the weekend. There was no reason for her to mention that there were still a couple of rooms available at the hotel, or that she could always give her room to Natalie and bunk with Esmé down in the tack room. No reason at all.

"But I can't sleep here." Natalie's cheeks colored. "Surely, you can see that."

"Of course." Caitlin stood up and tucked her hands into the pockets of her well-worn jeans. "Certainly, I can see it. I mean, who knows what might happen if you and Gage had to share this room?"

Natalie's blush deepened. "Nothing would happen," she said briskly. "It's just that I'd rather not."

"As I said, Nat, I understand." Caitlin offered a woman-to-woman smile. "You don't love Gage anymore. And he doesn't love you. "Still..." Caitlin winked. "You're a woman, he's a man. You obviously find each other attractive—"

"Found," Natalie said quickly.

"That's what I meant. You *found* each other attractive, once upon a time. So, who knows? The pheromones might still be in the air."

"The what might still be in the air?"

"You know. The stuff that drew you together—physically—in the first place." Caitlin turned away and began fluff-ing the pillows on the bed. "And I can see where you certainly wouldn't want to let Gage, you know, think he could get you into bed again."

"That is the most ridiculous thing I ever heard! Gage couldn't get me into bed if he got down and begged."

"Sure. I understand. But he won't, when I tell him he's going to have to bunk in with Travis or Slade."

"What do you mean, he won't?"

"Oh, you know how men are." Caitlin arched her brows. "Gage has such a huge ego that as soon as I tell him you won't share a room with him, he'll figure it's because you don't trust yourself."

"Trust myself?"

"Uh huh. Trust yourself."

Natalie huffed out a breath. "That," she said, "is altogether ridiculous."

It certainly was, but Caitlin figured she was on a roll. Dazzle 'em with talk and go easy on the facts. She'd heard Jonas say that a dozen times to explain how he managed to make so many brilliant deals. And that was just what she was doing, now.

"*I* know you won't let him near you. *You* know you won't let him near you. And we both know he'll have to spend the night on the *chaise longue* in the dressing room." She sighed. "But Gage won't know a thing. He'll tell himself, and Trav, and Slade, and anybody else who'll listen, that you're still crazy about him, that you don't trust yourself to share a room with him. By tomorrow morning, speculation about your sex life—or your supposed lack of a sex life—will be the topic of the hour. Why, I can just hear Jonas, at that breakfast buffet for sixty, telling everybody who'll listen exactly how—"

"Forget putting Gage in with his brothers," Natalie snapped. "The skunk'll stay right here, tying to fit himself onto a couch half his size, while I sleep the sleep of the righteous, in that bed."

"Are you sure that's what you want to do?" Caitlin said, trying not to sound smug.

"I'm positive." Natalie slung her carry-on onto the bed

and opened it. "Were you serious about lending me something to wear?"

"Of course."

"Good." She smiled grimly. "I just hope you've got something slinky that fits me, Catie. I'm going to give that man exactly what he deserves, the sight of his dressed-for-sin wife flirting with half the men here and then telling him it's hands-off once the lights are out. I'm going to send that man's libido into hyperspace."

Caitlin laughed and held out her hand. "Let's go take a look."

"Let's," Natalie said, and it wasn't until hours later that she realized that sending Gage's libido into hyperspace had probably not been the best of ideas.

By seven-thirty, most of the guests had arrived.

By eight, a crowd glittery enough to have been at home in any of the world's major cities had collected in the living room, overflowed into the library, and pushed out onto the three-level terrace.

It was a scene that reminded Gage all too clearly of the night at the Holcombs's. The mob of people, the canapés, the wine, the standing around and waiting—

Waiting for the ax to fall.

Sooner or later, his wife had to put in an appearance, and only a miracle would keep her from trying to kill him.

He hadn't seen Natalie all afternoon. He, his brothers and Grant had stayed in the hayloft for a while, talking about life in general, women in particular, and the amazing circumstances that had brought Grant to Espada.

"One of my partners," Grant had said, "a guy named Sam Abraham, handled your father's affairs for years. Sam retired a couple of months back, and I took over."

"Well," Travis had said, "it's just great that you came down for the party. Is your wife with you?"

Grant had looked down at his hands, cleared his throat and muttered something about how it was great, wasn't it, and yeah, Crista was with him and, uh, and he figured maybe being away together for a couple of days would be a pretty good thing.

Just about then, Caitlin had come along, looking for Slade. Travis had wandered off, and Gage had figured he'd use his time alone with Grant to tell him that he'd thought of calling him when he'd figured he'd need a lawyer.

"But I've changed my mind," he'd said as the two of them stood leaning against a fence. "I don't intend to let Natalie divorce me, dammit. I still love her, and I'm not convinced... Grant? Are you listening?"

"Sure," Grant had replied, and then he'd sighed and launched into his own tale of woe, which seemed to involve a gorgeous wife, a scruffy mongrel dog, a cat and twin daughters, Jessamyn and Jennifer. He'd produced a photo of two adorable babies seated in the lap of an exotic-looking brunette.

"My wife, Crista," Grant said, and then he cleared his throat, hard. "She says I don't understand her."

And then the two of them had swapped stories that only proved that Crista was right because how could any rational man ever hope to understand an irrational, emotional, impossible-to-please female?

Eventually, Grant's wife had come looking for him. She was gorgeous, all right, but Gage didn't have to be a genius to see that she treated Grant the same polite, impersonal way Natalie had treated him the past few months.

"Time to change for dinner," Crista had said after introductions, and Grant had gone back to the house with her.

Gage had gone back, too. His bedroom had been empty, but Natalie's suitcase was there, and the faint trace of her perfume.

He'd showered and put on his tux—twice in less than a month was more than enough for any man—and he'd tried not to put any special significance in the fact that Natalie hadn't barricaded the bedroom door or left his things in the hall.

So now here he was, playing hide-and-seek with a potted cactus instead of a potted palm, slugging down vintage Krug instead of bubbly that had gone into the plant container last time, doing his damnedest to look casual while he searched for Natalie.

He'd done his best, while he was dressing, not to think about the fact that she probably didn't have anything to wear except that funereal-looking suit. Not that it would matter. In this high-priced assemblage of designer silk, satin, and Shalimar, his wife—his beautiful wife—would make heads turn no matter what she wore.

On the other hand, she might not show up. She might just hole up in their room. At least she hadn't left Espada; a discreet inquiry to Caitlin had assured him of that.

"Have you seen Natalie anywhere?" he'd asked, and Catie had smiled sweetly and said yes, she had, and she was sure Nat would be along any second.

Okay. But the seconds had stretched into minutes, the minutes into a quarter hour, and now...

And now, Gage thought, while his heart tripped into overdrive, now, there she was.

No wrinkled suit for Natalie. His wife—his magnificent wife—was wearing an emerald-green dress. It started low and ended high, and for one wild minute he wanted to race across the room, tear off his jacket and wrap her inside it because no man but he had the right to see so much of her beautiful body. She was wearing a pair of heels that made the ones she'd worn at the Holcomb party look innocent, and she'd done something to her hair. It looked as if a man might have run his hands through it after a long night in bed.

Gage's fingers tightened around the champagne flute.

She wasn't just beautiful. She was hot, hot as a blowtorch.

And she was his.

"Natalie," he said softly, and, as if she'd heard him, Natalie's head came up and her gaze swept the room.

Gage's body tightened and became like stone. It was as if time were running backwards. The party. The crowd. Natalie, standing alone, searching the room...

Searching it for him.

He ditched his drink, took a deep breath and stepped out

from behind the cactus. Their eyes met, and Natalie—oh, yes, Natalie smiled.

"Natalie," he said again, and started towards her, knifing through the crowd, ignoring everything and everyone, even the sound of Jonas's voice and then Travis's.

"Natalie," he whispered just as he reached her...

"Senator," she said, and brushed past him. "How lovely to see you again."

Gage swung around. His wife was gazing up into the ruggedly handsome face of a man the papers often referred to as Washington's Most Eligible Bachelor. The guy had stayed at the Windsong a couple of times; Natalie had always treated him pleasantly enough but now she was looking at him as if he were Romeo and she were Juliet.

"Mrs. Baron, my dear." The senator took her hand and raised it to his lips. "How beautiful you look. And what a charming surprise this is. I never considered that you might be related to Jonas Baron."

Natalie tossed her head in a way that made Gage's blood pressure begin to climb.

"It's a lovely surprise for me, too. I didn't realize you and my father-in-law were friends." She smiled. "And please, do call me Natalie."

"I'd be delighted." The senator grinned. "So long as you call me John."

"John. Of course."

"And where is that husband of yours this evening, Natalie?"

Gage opened his mouth. I'm right here, he started to say... But Natalie cut him off with a girlish laugh.

"I've no idea," she said. "And I'm feeling quite neglected. Would you believe I hadn't even had a sip of champagne?"

"No," the senator said in mock horror.

"Yes," Natalie said, with another trilling laugh. "Isn't that awful?"

"It's terrible." He took her hand and looped it through his arm. "And I intend to remedy the situation immediately, Natalie."

"Please do, John," she replied.

And, just like that, they faded into the crowd and were gone.

Gage told himself to take it easy. Natalie was an adult. She could talk with whomever she liked, go off for champagne with whomever she liked...

...Flirt with whomever she liked, the Tulip boy for starters, and now a guy known as much for his philandering as for his politics?

"No," he muttered. "Hell, no. She can't."

"Talkin' to yourself, boy?"

Gage blinked. Jonas had come up beside him, with Marta on his arm. She smiled pleasantly. Jonas smirked.

"Father," Gage said. "You'll have to excuse me. I'm—"

"Never run after a woman, boy. Haven't you learned that by now?"

Gage's eyes narrowed. "With all due respect to you, Marta," he said, and looked straight at Jonas. "You're hardly a man to give advice about women, Father."

Jonas chuckled. "Because I've had five wives? Hell, Gage, that just gives me some perspective. Don't run after her, is my advice. Not unless you want her to have the pleasure of seein' just how bad off you are."

Marta leaned over and kissed Gage's cheek just before Jonas led her away.

"I know you don't want to believe him," she whispered, "but he's right."

Gage's jaw tightened as he stared after his father and Marta. How could Jonas be right? He'd never managed to keep a wife.

Hell, he thought miserably, who was he to criticize the old man's record? From the way things looked, he wasn't doing much of a job of keeping the only wife he'd ever had.

"Champagne, sir?"

Gage looked at the waiter, then at the tray filled with glasses.

"Yeah," he said, "why not?"

What could he lose if he took Jonas's advice? It was obvious that Natalie was determined to give him the cold shoulder. Well, let her. Let her flirt her tousled head off.

He drank the bubbling wine in one gulp, hurried after the waiter and traded his empty glass for a full one.

When the night ended, when the lights went out, when the house was finally silent, Natalie would be in his room.

In his bed.

And then, oh, yes, then he'd take her in his arms and show her exactly who it was she belonged to.

It was a great plan, but by midnight, he'd given it up.

His head hurt. His disposition would have sent a grizzly running. And after watching Natalie smile and flirt with nearly every man in the room, Gage had decided he just didn't give a damn. She wanted those other jerks instead of him? Fine. Let her have them.

Who was he kidding? Gage thought bitterly as he climbed the steps to his bedroom. This marriage was finished. Tomorrow morning, first thing, he'd tell that to his brothers, and to Grant.

He'd spoken only one sentence to Natalie all evening.

"Where are you sleeping tonight?" he'd said coldly, after catching up to her for the one moment she'd been alone.

"Don't you mean, with whom?" she'd said just as coldly. "I can tell you one thing, Gage. It won't be with you."

"Fine," he'd snarled, and stalked off.

She could sleep with every man in the State of Texas, he'd told himself…but he knew he didn't really mean it. There were rules, dammit, and one rule sure was that a woman didn't sleep with one man while she was still married to another—especially if the woman was his wife.

So he'd sidled over to Caitlin.

"I suppose you know Natalie and I are having problems," he'd said gruffly.

Catie had nodded and put a gentle hand on his. "Yes. And I'm sorry about it."

That, at least, had brought a smile to his lips. "I know you are," he'd said, and then, because it had to be asked, he'd cleared his throat. "Did you, ah, did you make some arrangements for tonight? Sleeping arrangements, I mean. Because Natalie and I certainly can't share the same room. So, I thought, maybe, you might put her in with you."

Catie had smiled and kissed his cheek. "Dear Gage," she'd said softly, "stop worrying. Natalie and I took care of all that, first thing."

At least he didn't have to spend the night wondering about that, Gage thought as he opened his bedroom door.

The room was dark as pitch. The light switch was right here, on the wall...

No. His head was throbbing like a drum. The light would only make it worse. Mrs. Jonas Baron Number Three, or maybe Four, had refurnished the entire house. Gone was the narrow bed of his boyhood, but the setup was still familiar. He could find his way around the room in the dark.

Gage kicked off his shoes, stripped off his tux, peeled off his briefs and his socks and headed into the bathroom.

Natalie wanted to be free? She wanted to play games with all those jerks?

"Fine," he muttered around a mouthful of toothpaste. "That's just fine with me."

She could have them. And they could have her. Don't chase after a woman, Jonas had said, but tonight Gage had tacked on an addendum. Don't chase after a woman who doesn't want you, especially when there were plenty who did.

Maybe it was time to start looking around.

He shut off the water, dried his hands and face and got into bed, then lay down, his hands clasped beneath his head.

He'd gone back and forth with this thing like one of those balls he used to have when he was a kid, the kind that was attached to a paddle by a rubber band. Well, all that shilly-shallying was over. He wanted out. Natalie wanted out. And the sooner it happened, the better.

Gage yawned, punched the pillow, and fell asleep.

It wasn't easy, being a full-time flirt.

Natalie sighed as she climbed the stairs to her room.

She'd sipped champagne with the senator, dined with a hunky heartthrob from Hollywood, danced with a media mogul and oohed at the fireworks with an admiring TV anchorman. And all the time she was smiling and laughing and making an ass of herself, she'd been aware of Gage, lurking in the shadows.

Lord, her feet hurt. Well, no wonder. They, and the dress Caitlin had lent her, had both turned out to be a size too small.

"Your feet can suffer for one night," Caitlin had said. "As for the dress..." She'd laughed. "Every man who sees you is going to try to figure out how you got into it, and how he can get you out of it."

Gage had suffered. She'd known that from the second he'd spotted her. The nerve of him, thinking she'd been searching the room for him...although, angry and out of love with him as she was, that first glimpse of him, tall, dark and handsome in his tux, with all that heat in his eyes, had almost undone her.

Gage, she'd thought. Oh, Gage, I still—I still...

Natalie clucked her tongue as she made her way down the hall. She didn't "still" anything. Even if she did, what was the good of a marriage that didn't work? Gage had changed. Their relationship had changed. And the sooner they ended it, the better.

She stepped inside the bedroom and closed the door. The room was dark, except for a pale swath of moonlight that stretched from the window to the bathroom. She reached for the light switch, then hesitated. Why turn on the lights when she could see all she needed to see just fine? Her head ached, as much from the champagne as from the strain of the evening. And she probably had only a few minutes to get ready, before Gage put in an appearance.

The last she'd seen of him, he'd been standing on the patio, alone, arms folded, back stiff as a steel rod, with a face like granite.

She could just imagine that face when he got here and discovered he was going to spend the night curled on the dollhouse-size couch in the dressing room.

Natalie went into the bathroom, washed her face and brushed her teeth. Then she headed back into the bedroom and began to work the too small dress down over her hips. It was made of some kind of stretchy material; you had to tug and pull to get it down...

"Natalie?"

The light came on, as blinding as a flare. She gasped and threw her arm over her eyes.

"Natalie?" Gage said again, and she dropped her arm and stared across the room at her husband.

He was sitting up against the pillows with the blankets down around his hips. His hair was tousled, his jaw was shadowed, his chest was bare. He looked as sexy as she'd ever seen him...

And what in hell was he doing here?

"What in hell are you doing here?" she demanded.

Gage frowned. "What do you mean, what am I doing here? This is my room."

"I know it's your room. But you were downstairs, on the patio..."

But he wasn't on the patio now. He was here, and she was here. He was naked—he always slept naked. And she might as well have been, considering the wispy black bra she was wearing, the scrap of black lace, the black stockings and garter belt because, dammit, that was what Caitlin said Neiman Marcus had sent to wear with the dress...

"What are you looking at?" Natalie demanded.

Gage sat up straighter. What, indeed? His wife, that's what he was looking at. His sexy, beautiful wife, who had chosen not to spend the night in a spare room, who'd chosen not to spend it with one of the sleazy bastards who'd fawned all over her downstairs because...

Because she wanted him.

"I'm looking at you, babe," he said very softly, and in one easy motion, he tossed back the covers, rose from the bed, and started towards her.

Natalie's heart gave a thump. "Gage," she said. "Gage..."

Don't. That was what she intended to say, but how could she tell a lie?

Her throat constricted. The man coming towards her was her husband. Her handsome, virile husband, his blue eyes blazing with desire, his body fully, magnificently aroused.

He wanted her. And she—she wanted him. She always had, always would...

"Natalie," he whispered when he reached her.

She trembled as he reached out and cupped her face in his hands. He kissed her, gently at first, his lips barely brushing hers, and she made a soft, sweet sound in her throat that sent the blood surging though his veins.

"Tell me," he said thickly as he undid her bra. "Say it. I need to hear you say it."

Her head fell back as her breasts tumbled into his waiting hands. He bent and kissed the creamy slopes, the proud crests; he whispered her name as he eased the scrap of black lace down her hips.

"Tell me," he demanded as his eyes met hers again, and Natalie gave a choked sob and went into her husband's arms.

"Make love to me, Gage," she whispered. "Kiss me. Touch me. Come deep inside me..."

Gage groaned, swung his wife into his arms, carried her to the bed and took what had always been, what surely always would be, his.

CHAPTER SEVEN

NATALIE awoke to the warmth of the sun and the heat of her husband's arms.

The night they'd spent flashed before her like a dream. A wonderful dream, overflowing with passion, and with love.

Oh, it was a miracle! Here she was, locked in Gage's embrace again, dizzy with feelings she'd all but forgotten...

"Good morning, wife."

She smiled dreamily as Gage turned on his side, his arms still holding her close.

"Good morning, husband."

He kissed her, his mouth gentle against hers.

"I had a wonderful dream last night."

"Really?" Natalie's lips curved against his. "What a coincidence. I had a wonderful dream, too."

Gage's hand slipped lightly down her back, cupped her bottom and drew her closer against him. The familiar heat and hardness of his aroused flesh pressed against her and she made a soft murmur of pleasure.

"Nice," she sighed.

Gage chuckled. "Wicked woman," he said, and moved against her.

"I meant," Natalie said, trying to sound prim but failing miserably, "it's nice we both had good dreams."

"Uh-huh." He kissed her again, his tongue slipping between her parted lips. "I dreamed you and I made love. Is that what you dreamed?"

Her eyes drifted shut. "Yes. I had the same...oh. Oh," she whispered, her breath catching, "Gage..."

"Nat." His voice was a choked groan. "Babe, you feel so good. So right. So perfect, in my arms."

So good. So right. So perfect. Natalie buried her face in Gage's shoulder as he moved over her. That was how she felt, too. Making love with him had been wonderful. For the first time in more months than she wanted to count, it hadn't been only her body that had responded to his caresses, it had been her soul.

She couldn't remember the last time it had been like this between them. It had almost happened that night in the Holcombs's garden, but the feeling hadn't lasted.

Last night, it had.

She'd been on fire for Gage's kisses. For his touch. There'd been no time to think, to weigh if what she was doing was right or wrong, if she'd regret it the next day, if...

If!

Natalie's eyes flew open. "Gage."

"Mmm."

"Gage, wait."

"I have waited." He kissed her breast, slid his hand between her thighs. "I've waited weeks, Nat. Months. It hasn't been this way for a long, long time."

"That's what I mean." Natalie put her hands on her husband's shoulders and pushed him away. "We didn't use anything last night."

"Didn't use..."

"Yes. And we haven't done that since—since..."

Gage went still. "Since you lost the baby," he said, and rolled off her.

Natalie felt the coldness start in her heart and work its way through her blood. Since *you* lost *the* baby. Not, since *we* lost *our* baby, but why would he have said it that way? Why change it, when he'd been saying the same thing, the same way, from the day she'd miscarried?

"Yes." All at once, she felt exposed. Vulnerable. She reached for the sheet, dragged it up over herself and clutched it to her chin. What a fool she was! Could she really have thought that one night of passion would change things?

"That's right." Her voice was cool, almost toneless, mirroring the emptiness in her heart. "This is the first time we didn't use protection since I lost the baby."

Gage nodded. He sat up against the headboard, then looked

at his wife. A moment ago, she'd been lying beneath him, her body warm, naked and welcoming. Now she was covered from her toes to her chin, looking at him as if he were some unpleasant creature that had invaded her personal space.

A coldness settled in the pit of his belly. That look was on her face again, the look he'd sworn to himself, after she'd walked out of his life, he'd damn well never tolerate again.

"Meaning," he said, "you might have gotten yourself knocked up last night."

He knew well that the words were cruel and crude but he didn't care, not even when he saw Natalie flinch. She wasn't the only one who'd realized they'd made love without him wearing a condom. He'd thought of it the last time she'd gone into his arms, with dawn just breaking in the eastern sky. And the sudden realization that they might be creating a child— that Natalie *wanted* his child—had made the moment she'd shattered in his arms and he in hers, all the sweeter.

What a fool you are, Baron, he thought coldly, and swung his legs over the side of the bed.

Natalie tugged furiously at the sheet and wound it around herself as she sat up.

"What a charming way to put it," she said, her voice trembling. "But you needn't worry, Gage. Fortunately for us both, this is the wrong time of the month."

"And a damned good thing," he said as the weight in his belly moved up and became a lump of iron lodged in his heart. "The last thing we'd want is a child, Natalie. Isn't that right?"

Natalie got to her feet, the sheet wrapped tightly around her.

"Absolutely," she said, and slammed the bathroom door behind her.

Travis was seated at the dining room table when Gage came striding into the room.

"Good morning," he said.

Gage growled a response, poured himself a cup of coffee, and pulled out a chair.

Travis's brows lifted. "Somehow, I get the impression it isn't. A good morning, I mean."

Gage shot him a look. "I'm warning you right now, Travis, I am not in the mood for fun and games."

Travis nodded. Actually, neither was he. The weekend wasn't working out quite as he'd expected, but he had the feeling Gage wasn't in the mood to trade war stories. Besides, he wasn't really sure what kind of story he had to tell, or even if he wanted to tell it. Not yet.

"Well, let me make your mood worse by giving you the good news and the bad news." He rose from his chair, went to the sideboard and speared another waffle onto his plate. "The good news is we can blow off the formal brunch. The bad news is that we have a command performance with the old man in half an hour."

"The old man knows what he can do with his command performances."

"Yeah." Slade strolled into the dining room and headed for the sideboard. "I don't think he can get away with ordering us to muck out the stalls in the stable anymore, if we don't click our heels and salute."

"And don't you sound cheerful this morning," Gage said, looking up from his coffee.

"Do me a favor, okay? Just lay off the wisecracks." Slade stalked to the sideboard. "How're the waffles? Does Carmen still make them so light you have to hold 'em down with a fork?"

"Light as air," Travis said.

"And a good thing," Slade said darkly. "At least, some things don't change."

Travis and Gage looked at each other. After a minute, the three brothers tucked into their breakfasts. It wasn't long before Slade pushed his plate aside and reached for his coffee.

"So, Jonas wants to see us. Any idea what it's about?"

"Espada," Grant Landon said as he entered the room. "Morning, gentlemen. Is that breakfast laid out on that sideboard, or is it dinner for sixty?"

"I see you're trying for the casual look today, Landon." Gage smiled. "White shirt, gray suit...but no tie."

"Let me team you with my wife," Grant said coolly. "The two of you have enough material for a comedy routine."

Travis and Slade exchanged a look.

"Uh, try the waffles," Travis said. "And the homemade strawberry preserves. You'll think you died and went to heaven."

Silence settled over the room again. Then Slade cleared his throat. "You said the old man wants to discuss Espada, Landon? How would you know that?"

"He'd know it because he's Jonas's attorney." Caitlin strode into the dining room, waved the men back into their chairs when they started to stand, and stole a strip of bacon from Slade's plate. "Jonas is worried about what's going to happen when he dies. Isn't that right, Grant?"

"You've got it." Grant split open a biscuit and loaded it with strawberry jam. "He's asked me to assure you that you'll all share equally in the Baron holdings."

"All four of us," Travis said firmly, looking at his stepsister.

"All four, yes. Jonas was very clear about that." A smile softened Grant's hard mouth. "He thinks of Caitlin as his daughter." The smile faded. "Except with regard to Espada."

Gage looked up and frowned. "What's that supposed to mean?"

"It means," Caitlin said quietly, "that Jonas will only leave the ranch to someone who has Baron blood." A rueful smile slid over her lips. "And that leaves me out."

"But you love this place," Gage said.

"I do." She smiled tightly. "But I'm not a Baron."

"That's ridiculous." Travis shoved back his chair. "Every one of us but Catie chose to leave Espada and make a life elsewhere, and I'd bet my last buck not a one of us would be willing to come back."

"Right," Slade and Gage said in what might have been one voice.

"You see, Landon? Our sister's the only one who gives a damn about the ranch."

"I agree. But take it from me, gentlemen—and lady," Grant added with a nod in Caitlin's direction. "Men like your father make unilateral decisions that don't fit any logic but their own. And this isn't Grant Landon, Esquire, talking, guys, it's Grant Landon, offspring of a tough old S.O.B. who ran his own corner of the world pretty much the way Jonas does."

Gage rose, walked to Caitlin's side and put his arm around her. "Well, the old man will just have to change his plans."

"He won't." Grant shrugged. "He'll leave Espada to his nephew, if none of you will tell him what he wants to hear."

"To Leighton?" Travis snorted. "That man's as sneaky as a snake."

"And lower than its belly," Slade added.

"This is just ridiculous," Gage said sharply. "And it sure as hell isn't fair." He paused, then gave a hollow laugh. "On the other hand, neither is life."

"Damn right," Grant muttered.

Silence fell over the room again. This time, it remained unbroken.

Natalie hadn't made a sound during the time it had taken Gage to dress and leave the bedroom.

She'd stood plastered against the bathroom door, listening, not drawing an easy breath until, at last, she heard the door slam shut after him.

"You idiot," she said as she turned to the mirror.

What in hell had she been thinking of, to have slept with him?

Natalie blew a strand of hair out of her eyes. That was just the trouble. She hadn't been thinking. Otherwise, she'd never have had sex with Gage. And that was what they'd done, she thought grimly as she turned on the shower, they'd had sex. They'd screwed. Even thinking the word made her flinch but, dammit, there was no way she'd go on pretending that what they'd done had anything to do with making love.

It hadn't, for a long time.

Gage still wanted her, still found her an attractive turn-on, but that was all that remained of their relationship. And, as he'd just reminded her, losing the baby had only confirmed it.

God, the despair of that day. Her sobs. Her anguish. Her need for the comfort of Gage's arms. But he'd been out of town, as usual, on some big business deal, as usual, and she had been alone... She made a wry face at herself in the mirror. All alone, as usual.

Natalie wrapped herself in a towel and walked slowly into the bedroom.

She'd been alone, one way or another, during her pregnancy, too. Gage had been in the middle of overseeing the construction of a hotel.

"Uh-huh," he'd say when she'd ask him about nursery wallpaper or cribs or colors. "Right. Whatever you like, Nat. Check with the decorator, why don't you?"

Natalie pulled on her clothes.

Eventually, she'd figured out that he wasn't just busy, he was disinterested. Men were like that, Liz Holcomb said, but Gage wasn't "men," he was her husband. And he was going to be the father of her child...

And then, he wasn't.

She woke up one morning, started to dress, felt a sudden cramp and it was over.

The baby was gone.

Her heart, her body, were empty.

"I'm so sorry you lost the baby, Nat," Gage had said.

Sorry. That was the best he could come up with, when her heart had been breaking. When *his* heart should have been breaking, too, but then, it was *the* baby she'd lost, not *our* baby.

Oh, how she'd hated him at that moment!

But she hadn't shown it. She'd thanked him, politely, for his concern, and watched him take up his life again as if nothing had happened. He never thought of or mentioned the baby again. It was as if she'd never carried their child inside her. And that was when she'd finally realized that he'd never wanted the baby at all.

A baby would have interfered with the life they'd led before she got pregnant. The traveling, the parties, the racing around the globe from one Baron resort to another. It would have ruined their perfect house, with its perfect furnishings, its perfect decorations.

Natalie closed her suitcase.

That life had gone on, but with subtle changes. For one thing, she'd stopped traveling with Gage. She was, she said, too busy.

And she was busy. She joined clubs, served on charity boards, played tennis until she hated the sight of the racquet and the net, but Gage didn't notice. Or, if he did, he didn't care. He didn't need her anymore.

It had been different, years ago. He used to hurry home to her, then, take her in his arms and swing her off her feet.

"I missed you," he'd say, and she'd believed it, because she missed him, too, even when they'd only been apart for the day.

Then he'd tasted success. And, so gradually that she hadn't realized it was happening until it was too late, his need for her had changed. She became a well-dressed, well-groomed trophy, the walking, talking proof of her husband's dream of achievement—a dream that had no room for children.

Now, it had no room for her.

Natalie rubbed the back of her hand over her eyes, then picked up her carry-on.

"Goodbye, Gage," she said to the empty room.

This time, she was walking out of his life forever.

Unfortunately, escape wasn't quite that simple.

Abel, who'd managed the ranch for as long as anybody could remember, pulled off his hat, scratched his head, spat in the dirt and finally confirmed what she'd already figured out for herself.

"Ain't nothin' around but the tractors, Miz Natalie," he

said. "Mr. Jonas's guests done commandeered purty near ever'thin' with wheels."

Trapped, Natalie thought as she made her way back to the house, trapped like an animal in a cage.

She trotted up the steps to the back porch, warily opened the door to the kitchen, and breathed a sigh of relief that it was empty. The yeasty aroma of fresh bread hung in the air, and a pot of coffee stood on the corner counter. Natalie poured some into a mug, went out the door again, and leaned her elbows on the porch railing. She could feel her anger giving way, turning into something else, something that made her feel weepy.

"Damn," she whispered, "damn, damn, damn!"

"Is the coffee that bad?"

Natalie whirled around. Marta Baron had just stepped onto the porch. She had a cup in her hand and was smiling.

"No," Natalie said, and dredged up a smile in return. "I was just—I was—"

"No need to explain," Marta said. She stepped aside as another woman came out onto the porch. The woman was young and beautiful, with hair as black as the night. Her skirt seemed to be made of a thousand different colors, all of them complimented by a crimson jersey top. Tiny silver bells hung from her ears.

Marta smiled at Natalie. "I just didn't want Crista to think I'd been lying about what superb coffee Carmen makes."

"It's true. Carmen's coffee is wonderful." Natalie cleared her throat. "I was just…I was thinking."

Marta nodded. "There seems to be a lot of that in the air today," she said, smiling. "For instance, I just found Crista doing the same thing in the library."

The woman with the silver bell earrings laughed. "Mrs. Baron's being kind. What she means is that I was muttering to myself."

"Birds of a feather," Natalie said, and offered a real smile. She held out her hand. "Natalie Baron."

"Crista Landon," Crista said. "It's very nice to meet you."

Marta glanced at her watch. "Would you both excuse me? I detoured to get some coffee for Crista and me, but I'm supposed to be rounding up Mr. Landon and Jonas's sons, and herding them into the library."

Natalie grinned. "I see you've picked up Texas lingo."

Marta rolled her eyes. "When in Rome," she said, and the door swung shut after her.

"Well," Crista said.

"Well," Natalie said.

They leaned their elbows on the porch railing and gazed out over Espada's rolling landscape.

Crista sighed. "How peaceful it is."

Natalie nodded in agreement. "Yes, it is."

"It's one of the reasons I agreed to fly down with Grant. My husband," Crista said, and touched the tip of her tongue to her lips. "I, ah, I thought, perhaps, it might be nice if we got away from things for a while, if we spent the weekend alone, without the children."

"Children?"

"Uh-huh. We have twins." Crista smiled. "Two little girls."

"Oh, how nice."

"Yes, they're the joy of my life." Crista's smile dimmed. "Still, I thought, if Grant and I just took a few days alone..."

"Yes?"

"Oh, I don't know. I guess I had some silly idea we might patch up our troubles..." Her gaze flew to Natalie and she blushed. "Sorry. I don't know why I said that. I mean, I'm not in the habit of dumping my problems on people, especially strangers."

"I guess there are times it can be a good idea." Natalie pushed a windblown strand of hair behind her ear. "Strangers aren't as judgmental as friends or relatives."

"My husband wouldn't agree. He'd say I'm too trusting."

"Take it from me," Natalie said grimly, "being too trusting can be a big mistake."

Crista sighed. "I suppose you're right."

"I know I am. If I'd listened to my own advice, I wouldn't even be here."

"I don't follow that."

Natalie blew out a breath. "Let's put it this way," she said. "At least you came here willingly."

Crista turned and stared at Natalie, her eyes widening. "Didn't you?"

"My husband—I'm married to Gage Baron—my husband damn near kidnapped me."

"That sounds romantic."

"Believe me, it wasn't. He lied, said his father was dying…well, he intimated it."

"Why on earth would he do that?"

"To get his own way." Natalie took a sip of coffee. "Gage would have said anything, just about then. He was angry as hell."

"Why?" Crista blushed again. "Oh, Natalie, I'm sorry. I don't mean to pry, it's just that—"

"That's all right. There's no need to keep it quiet any longer. Gage was angry because he saw that I was capable of making a life that doesn't center on him."

Crista gave a deep sigh. "Sounds like my husband. 'Where have you been, Crista? Who were you with, Crista?' He's an attorney and I swear, sometimes I feel as if he's got me on the witness stand."

"Doesn't he trust you?"

"There was a time I'd have said he'd trust me with his life, but lately…"

"Lately?"

Crista shrugged. "We come from very different backgrounds. And I think Grant's afraid that I find our life dull."

"Do you?"

"No. Oh, no! I wouldn't change a thing about it… But that doesn't mean I don't want to kick up my heels once in while. And that upsets him. He can't see why I'd want to go down to the Village—Greenwich Village, in New York—touch bases with old friends, see what kind of jewelry is popular, now that I've closed my shop."

"Your shop?"

"Uh-huh. I used to have this little store where I made and sold my own designs. Silver, mostly, though I've done some work in gold, too. Grant thought it took too much of my time…" Crista laughed. "Just look at me, telling you the story of my life. What about you? Your husband owns a bunch of hotels, doesn't he? I'll bet you lead a glamorous life."

Natalie looked down into her coffee. "I left my husband," she said softly.

"Oh, Natalie…"

"It's okay. I mean, it's not, but there was nothing else I could do once I realized that—that what we once had was over."

Crista put her hand over Natalie's. "I'm so sorry."

"Yes. I am, too. But there's no use denying the truth. Gage and I are finished. I don't understand the man he's become or the life he prefers. Perhaps, if we'd had a child…" Silence fell between the women. After a while, Natalie cleared her throat. "So," she said briskly, "when do you and your husband fly back to New York?"

A shadow darkened Crista's eyes. "We were supposed to go back tomorrow."

"Supposed to?"

Crista nodded. "I'm not going back. I—I started to tell Grant this morning, but I think he knew what I was going to say. He walked out of the room before I could say it. The thing is, I need some time away from him, to think."

"But your daughters…"

"I phoned home. Their nanny is going to fly down to Palm Beach with my babies, and I—"

"Palm Beach? That's only an hour from where I live."

"Great! Maybe we can get together."

"But what's in Palm Beach?"

"My uncle's house. Well, it used to be my uncle's, but he left it to me. I couldn't think of anyplace else to go. The house is old and far too big for me and the twins, but it's right on the beach. It's quiet, and there's plenty of room for me to spread out and work. I really love working with my hands.'' She smiled. ''I never did make money at it, though, nothing much more than expenses. I'm the worst business-woman imaginable.''

''Well, I can't imagine being creative enough to draw a straight line.'' Natalie smiled. ''On the other hand, I've got a good head for business. I'd never have known it, until I got involved in all these charity things, but it turns out I'm a natural at organizing things and convincing people to buy stuff.'' She sighed, put her empty mug on a redwood table behind her, then tucked her hands into her pockets. ''I just wish I had a quiet place to go to, the way you do. A place where I could think, and sort out my life.''

''What's wrong with where you live?''

Natalie laughed. ''If you could see my apartment, you wouldn't ask. Gage thinks it's a hovel and I'd sooner die than let him know I agree. The bathroom ceiling leaks, the guy upstairs marches around wearing what have to be army boots, and the roaches are so big I'm almost afraid to step on them.''

Crista grinned. ''Sounds like my old place down in the Village. Too bad you can't...'' Her voice drifted to silence and then, suddenly, she swung towards Natalie. ''Natalie? Are you really a good saleswoman?''

Natalie grinned. ''Ask the Have a Heart Fund. Or the Children's Center. Or the Home for Animals. I raised zillions of bucks for—''

''The Home for Animals? You like animals, you mean?''

''I love them.'' Natalie sighed. ''We've never had any, though. I always wanted to, but we used to travel so much...''

Crista grabbed Natalie's hands. ''Come with me.''

''Come with you?'' Natalie said blankly. ''Come with you, where?''

''To Palm Beach. Don't shake your head, not until you've heard me out.''

''Crista, really—''

''The house is huge. You can have your own suite.''

''Yes, but—''

"I know we've just met, but, I don't know, I feel a kinship. Don't you feel it, too?"

Natalie bit her lip. "Yes. Yes, I do. But I have no money. I couldn't possibly pay you for—"

"Nonsense! I don't need your money, I need your friendship." Crista smiled. "Besides, I have an ulterior motive."

"You do?"

"Sure. You can deal with the business end of the jewelry thing."

"I don't know a thing about jewelry," Natalie said, but she could feel the excitement beginning to build inside her.

"You don't have to." Crista rolled her eyes. "There are all these la-di-da shops on Worth Avenue. I just know they'd carry my stuff, if I could figure out how to approach them, but people who move in that world look at somebody like me and don't know what to make of her. You, on the other hand, could just sashay right through those doors."

Natalie laughed. "Have you taken a good look at me, Crista?"

"Uh-huh. The suit looks like you slept in it...but the cut says 'Paris label.' And you wear it as if you were born to it." Crista waved her hand. "I can tell, Natalie. You have the right look. And I'd just bet you have the drive. The voice. The chutzpah." She grinned. "That's New Yorkese for the absolute brass it takes to make a good salesperson. I'm telling you, you'd fit right in."

Natalie hesitated. "I don't know," she said slowly. "A move to Palm Beach is a big step."

"Why? You said you've left your husband. You said Palm Beach is just an hour from where you live now. You said you need a place where you can think, where you can try and get yourself together..."

"We may feel some sort of kinship, but really, we don't even know each other."

Crista smiled. "What do you want to know? I told you, I have two daughters. You'll have to be prepared to have them drive you just a little bit crazy. They're at that stage where they love to babble, and get into all kinds of trouble."

"They sound wonderful."

"They are. Oh, and I have a cat, too."

"A cat," Natalie said, and smiled.

"And a dog. The dog'll be under your feet and the cat'll probably want to spend most of the day in your lap."

Natalie's smile broadened. "Sounds like pure torture."

"It is." Crista grinned. "So, what do you say? Is it a deal?"

"It's crazy," Natalie said, and laughed. "Absolutely crazy. And you know what? I think I'm going to love it."

"Going to love what?" a gruff voice said.

The women swung around. Gage and Grant were standing in the open doorway.

"Going to love what?" Gage repeated, and scowled.

Natalie's hand tightened on Crista's. "I'm giving up my apartment."

Gage felt a joy so intense it almost stole his breath away. "Babe," he said, and stepped forward. "Babe, that's wonderful. I knew you'd see reason, if you just—"

"I'm moving to Palm Beach."

"Palm...?" He felt the blood draining from his face. "What the hell are you talking about, Natalie?"

"Crista's asked me to move in with her."

Grant's handsome face went as white as Gage's. "Palm Beach? My wife asked you to... Crista? What in hell is she talking about?"

"I tried to tell you this morning," Crista said softly. "I'm not going back to New York, Grant. I've already spoken with Addie. She's flying down with the twins. With Annie and Sweetness, too. I need—"

"You need?" Grant's voice was ragged with tightly suppressed anger. "What about what I need, Crista? And I'll tell you right now, you are not taking my daughters from me."

"I would never do that. I'm not leaving you, Grant, I just need some time to think. And it'll be easier for everybody if the twins are with me."

"Easier for everybody," Grant said through his teeth. He

swung towards Gage. "Is this easier for you, Baron? To be told that our wives are going to set up house without us?"

Gage stared at Natalie. Her cheeks were bright with color, her chin tilted in defiance. She looked more beautiful than he had ever seen her, and more determined. He thought of last night, and how the heat of her had all but melted his bones, and a terrible sense of dread swept through his blood.

He moved forward, until they were a breath apart. "If you do this," he said softly, "it will really be all over."

Tears glittered in Natalie's eyes. "It was all over a long time ago."

Gage stepped back. She was right, and he knew it. And that was what hurt the most.

CHAPTER EIGHT

IT WAS going to be an adventure.

At least, that was what Natalie told herself while she waited for Crista to pack her things.

An adventure. And an exciting one.

She'd gone from being daughter to wife without so much as a breath in between. These few weeks were the first time she'd lived on her own but what she was about to do now— moving to a different city, plunging into a business she'd have to learn from the ground up—would really be burning her bridges behind her.

From now on, she'd be responsible to herself and for herself. That was what she needed. More than Crista, probably. From the looks of things, the Landon marriage had a very good chance of surviving.

Natalie pushed the kitchen door open, went to the stove and refilled her coffee mug.

A better than good chance, considering Grant's reaction to Crista's announcement.

"I won't let you do this," he'd said.

"You can't stop me," Crista had replied, and then she'd looked towards Natalie. "I'll be down in a minute."

"Don't count on it," Grant had snapped, and Crista had stormed into the house with her husband hard on her heels, his face set in angry lines, his voice rising as they disappeared up the stairs.

Natalie stepped out on the porch again and lifted her mug to her lips.

Watching him, hearing him, had put a lump in her throat. Grant loved his wife; any fool could see that he didn't want to lose her. But Gage...

The mug shook in Natalie's hand. She set it down carefully

on the railing, hugged her shoulders, and stared out blindly over Espada.

Gage hadn't done a thing. He hadn't begged or pleaded, hadn't lost his temper. He'd just stood looking at her impassively, delivered that quiet message of warning, and walked off after she'd refused to back down. Walked off, as if her leaving him was just an inconvenience he'd have to deal with.

For one wild moment, she'd come close to going after him. Damn you, Gage, she'd almost said, what's the matter with you? Are you just going to let me march out of your life without a word?

But sanity had prevailed, and thank goodness it had. She hadn't made a fool of herself by running after him. The truth was, Gage didn't *want* to try and stop her. Their marriage was over. The divorce would only make it a fact.

Tears blurred her vision. Oh, but she'd wanted him to say something. He should have looked the way Crista's husband had looked, as if the thought of losing his wife was going to break his heart.

Dammit, he should have cared!

"Ready?"

Natalie looked around. Crista was standing in the doorway, holding a small overnight bag. Her cheeks were flushed and her eyes looked unnaturally bright, as if she'd been crying. Grant stood behind her, arms folded, his body language humming with tightly controlled fury.

"Yes," Natalie said. "I'm ready. But I just remembered…there aren't any cars available to take us to the airport. I checked earlier."

Crista gave a faint smile. "I phoned for a taxi."

A taxi. It had been as simple as that. Natalie shivered. What kind of idiot was she that the thought of phoning for a cab hadn't occurred to her?

An idiot who really didn't want to leave her husband, perhaps?

"Natalie?"

Natalie blinked.

"The cab's out front."

Natalie took a deep breath. "Yes," she said, and without saying goodbye to anyone, without looking back, she followed Crista through the house, out the door, and into the waiting taxi.

Gage stepped out of the shadow of a cottonwood as the taxi pulled away.

"Go on, then," he muttered. "You want to leave me? Do it. See if I give a good…"

The harsh words caught in his throat. He swung away, eyes burning, face hot, hands knotted at his sides…and walked straight into the tall, lean figure of his father.

"Mornin'," Jonas said. "Pretty day."

Gage nodded and kept walking. Jonas fell in beside him.

"So," he said, "you don't want anythin' to do with Espada, is that right, boy?"

Gage drew a deep breath. "We had this conversation half an hour ago, Father. I told you then, I have—"

"—A life elsewhere." Jonas chuckled. "Can't blame a man for tryin', right?"

"Right," Gage said, and lengthened his stride. His father lengthened his, too.

"Headin' for the stables?"

Heading for hell, Gage thought. "Not really. I'm just taking a walk."

Jonas nodded, tucked his hands into his pockets and slid a glance at his son.

"She left you, did she?"

Gage stopped and swung towards the old man, his shoulders hunched.

"It's none of your business what she did," he said in a low voice. "When I was a kid, maybe, you could poke your nose into my affairs, tell me that Natalie was wrong for me, but—"

"Whoa, son." Jonas held up his hands. "That was more'n ten years ago."

"Look, what happens between my wife and me isn't up for discussion, okay?"

"Okay."

Gage began walking, more quickly this time, but that didn't stop Jonas, whose long legs made the pace seem easy.

"Actually, I figured it might be time to let you know I was wrong."

Gage swung towards him again. "Jonas Baron? Wrong?" He laughed. "What is this, Father? Are you turning over a new leaf after eighty-five years?"

Jonas put his hands in his pockets and rocked back on his booted heels.

"I figured Natalie was looking for a way out when she took up with you back then. It was no secret her father was a miserable, mean-spirited son of a bitch. And then there was all the Baron money, too."

"Yeah," Gage said grimly, "well, you were wrong. Natalie and I never touched a dime of the Baron money, now, did we?"

"Nope." A smile cracked Jonas's weather-beaten face. "You made it on your own, boy."

"My, oh, my. A red-letter day. Jonas Baron admits he made a mistake and gives his son the closest thing to a compliment anybody's ever heard."

"Natalie turned out to be a fine woman."

Gage slapped his hand to his forehead. "Great God Almighty, I'm not up for this! Another one? I wish I'd brought a tape recorder."

"And," Jonas said, refusing to rise to the bait, "you love her."

"You don't know a thing about me, or what I do or don't..." Gage's mouth twisted. "Ah, hell," he said. "Yeah. All right. I do. What now, Pop? You going to twist the knife, point out that for all my loving her, my wife has left me anyway?"

Jonas started walking towards the stables again. After a minute, Gage fell in beside him.

"I had a woman I loved like that," Jonas said softly. "A long, long time ago."

Gage looked at him in amazement. "Did you?"

"She was my heart and soul, boy, my heart and soul."

"Was she…" Gage cleared his throat. "Was she my mother? Our mother, Trav's and Slade's and mine?"

The old man sighed. "Your mother was a good woman. A wonderful woman. And I loved her." He looked down, kicked a clod of dirt out of the way. "But the woman I'm talkin' about was all I ever wanted out of this life."

Gage waited for his father to say more, but Jonas had fallen silent. They had reached the stables, where one of the ranch hands waited, his hand on the bridle of an enormous black stallion. Jonas took the bridle and waved the man away.

"And?" Gage said.

The stallion inside arched his midnight-dark neck and blew through its nostrils.

"And," Jonas said in a voice so low Gage had to strain to hear it, "I gave her everythin'. Everythin', boy. Even Espada. I built all this for her…but she wanted more."

"What?" Gage said. "What more did she want?"

The old man looked at him, his silver eyes suddenly gone dark.

"I never knew," he said. "She never said—and I had too much pride to ask."

Jonas swung up into the saddle, dug his heels into the stallion's flanks, and rode off.

Crista's house was exactly as she'd described it.

It was on the ocean, it was pink, it was enormous, it was old and it needed work…and Natalie loved it on sight.

"It's an eyesore," Crista said cheerfully as the two of them strolled through the high-ceilinged rooms, their footsteps echoing hollowly against the hardwood floors.

"It is that," Natalie agreed. "It's so homely that you just have to love it."

"Uh-huh. Just like my dog, Annie. Wait until you see her. Her muzzle is all whiskers." She grinned and looped her arm through Natalie's. "I knew you and I were sisters under the skin the minute I saw you."

"Whoa." Natalie made a face. "If those little porcelain

figures in that breakfront are yours, I'm not so sure about that 'sisters under the skin' business.''

Crista laughed. ''They belonged to my uncle, and if you think this is bad, you should have seen his place in New York.'' The women climbed the stairs to the second floor. ''Choose your bedroom.''

''It doesn't matter. Any one will be fine.''

''Oh, come on.'' Crista took Natalie's hand and tugged her from one doorway to the other. ''Be honest, now. Would you rather have a cabbage rose carpet?''

Natalie laughed. ''Wow.''

''Or water-stained chartreuse silk walls?''

''Oh, boy.''

''And then there's what I call the barn. Comes complete with hot-and-cold running drafts.''

Natalie laughed again. ''Isn't there a bedroom with plain white walls?''

''Sure. But the ceiling leaks.''

''You're kidding.''

''No.'' Crista smiled, but her smile seemed forced. ''It leaks whenever it rains. Grant had it fixed before we were married, but every time they fix one leak, it leaks someplace else.''

''Well, I guess I'll go with the cabbage roses.''

''Good choice. I'll take the chartreuse walls, and we can put the twins in next door to me, with their nanny on the other side. I can use the kitchen as my workroom. It's the brightest room in the house, and there's this big old butcher-block table...'' Crista took Natalie's hands and gave her a wobbly grin. ''This is going to be fun.''

Who was kidding who? Natalie wondered, and flashed an even more wobbly smile in return.

Six weeks later, Natalie stepped out of one of the most exclusive jewelry shops on Worth Avenue and walked briskly towards her car.

''Afternoon, Ms. Baron.''

She looked up, smiled at the man who'd greeted her, and

thought how incredible it was that a vice president of one of the largest banks in Palm Beach should know her by name.

Bank presidents, not just vice presidents, had known her back in Miami, but that was because she'd been Gage Baron's wife. Here, she was Natalie Baron, with an identity all her own as sales rep for *Designs by Crista*. The two-woman operation was rapidly turning into a success. They'd even turned enough of a profit from their first month's sales to put a down payment on a car.

And, as Crista kept happily pointing out, this was Palm Beach's off-season.

"Just wait until winter," she'd said only that morning. "We'll be working twenty hours a day!"

Natalie smiled to herself as she reached the car and unlocked it. It looked as if Crista's prophecy was going to come true, and months ahead of schedule, thanks to the visit she'd just paid to *The Emperor's Emporium*. The owner of the exclusive little shop had sold out every Design by Crista. And now he had a special request, one that would surely put their fledgling business over the top.

Natalie tossed her leather briefcase on the seat beside her, took off her silk suit jacket, and lay it on top of the briefcase.

It felt good, knowing she'd had a hand in all this. She felt useful, and happy. And she never, ever thought about Gage or missed him or—or—

Her smile tilted.

Okay. That was still a problem. She *did* think of Gage, and when she did she felt…she felt…

Natalie took a deep breath. Then she checked for traffic, pulled away from the curb, and drove home.

The pink house was blessedly cool after the hot sun of summertime Florida.

"I'm back," Natalie called as she stepped inside the foyer.

A black and tan dog of indeterminate parentage came hurtling around the corner, followed by a gray cat with one mangled ear.

"Hi, guys," Natalie said, kneeling down and opening her arms to the twosome. "Where's the rest of the crew?"

"An'Na," two little voices cried, and Jessamyn and Jennifer Landon came toddling towards her, their faces wreathed in smiles.

Natalie gave Annie and Sweetness each one last, loving pat. Then she scooped Crista's daughters up in her arms.

"That's right," she said, laughing as Jess patted her face with sticky hands and Jenn gave her a big grin. "It's Aunt Nat, back from the salt mines. I missed you, too, my angels."

"Hellions, is more like it," Crista said as she came around the corner. But her smile softened her words, and when the twins saw her, they held out their chubby arms. She grinned, took them from Natalie, covered their faces with smacking kisses and then handed them over to Addie, who took one look at her charges and scowled.

"Into the bathroom with you," she said. "Land's sake, you girls are a mess."

The twins gurgled and tugged at their nanny's hair. Addie sighed, muttered something about how they could charm the birds out of the trees, and gave each child a hug as she carried them off.

"The salt mines, huh?" Crista said. "Was it a bad day?"

"Oh, definitely," Natalie said, suppressing a grin. "I only sold out everything I took with me."

Crista squealed. "You're kidding!"

"I'm dead serious."

"Wow. I really thought it was a fluke. Selling so well, last month. But maybe it wasn't. Maybe we've got something here. Maybe—"

"There's no 'maybe' about it, Crista. Your stuff is wonderful."

"And you're the world's best saleswoman."

"Yeah." Natalie chuckled. "An unbeatable combo." She hesitated, eyes twinkling. "Uh, you can work with precious stones, can't you? Diamonds, for instance."

"Well, sure. I mean, I could, but the cost... Until we're sure we can sell stuff like that..."

"We have a commission."

"A commission? Are you sure? Does this person know how expensive it—"

Natalie leaned forward and whispered a name in Crista's ear.

Crista gasped. "No!"

"Yes." Natalie headed for the kitchen with Crista on her heels. "And," she said, opening the refrigerator door and taking out an orange, "once somebody like that commissions a piece, you can bet your bottom dollar her society friends will, too." She bumped the door closed with her hip. "Maybe it's time I took a few samples and drove down to that mall in Boca Raton."

Crista took an orange segment from Natalie's hand. "Great! And what about considering some shops in Miami Beach, too? You know, along South Beach."

Natalie's smile dipped, then recovered. "Of course," she said brightly. "There's a world of potential *Designs by Crista* fans in South Beach. I should have thought of that myself."

"No," Crista said slowly, putting her hand on Natalie's arm. "No, you shouldn't. And I'm a jerk for even mentioning the place."

"Don't be silly. It's time we expanded. Didn't I just say as much?"

"Nat, I know you don't want to go back there."

"To Miami Beach?" Natalie's smile was brittle. "Hey, it's just a place."

"A place full of memories." Crista hesitated. "Has he called?"

Natalie looked at Crista. "Gage?" she said as if there might be some doubt. "No. Why would he? He said that my moving here would be the end, and I agreed with him. Why on earth should he call?"

Crista leaned back against the sink. "Maybe because he's still in love with you, the same as you're still in love with him."

Natalie gave a trilling laugh. "What a romantic you are, Crista! Gage isn't in love with me. He hasn't been, for a long time."

"And you? Are you still in love with him?"

The women's eyes met, Natalie turned away, dumped the orange peel in the trash and turned on the water in the sink.

"If I were, would I have left him? Would I have moved to another city? Would I be meeting with my lawyer next week to discuss the divorce?"

"I don't know," Crista said softly. "Would you?"

"What's the difference?" Natalie said after a moment. Her voice broke, and she cleared her throat. "It doesn't matter. What Gage and I had is over. He doesn't phone, he doesn't write... And neither do I. Why, I don't even think about him anymore."

"You dream about him," Crista said. "I hear you, sometimes, crying in your sleep."

Natalie blinked hard. Waking with tears on your cheeks was one thing. Weeping now, during the day, would be quite another.

"I don't."

"Yeah, Nat. You do. I was coming from the twins' room, and I heard you."

"Maybe you heard the ocean. Or the wind in the palm fronds."

"The thing is..." Crista said carefully, "the thing is, Nat, that maybe you and Gage need to sit down and talk."

Natalie wiped her hands on a towel. "There's nothing to talk about."

"There must be. What about finding ways to compromise? To get past the things that separate you?"

"He wants to own the world," Natalie said calmly. "And I just want to *be* his world. And to have a family to make our world complete. There's no room to get past those differences."

"Have you told him all of that?"

"There's no point in telling him anything. He's made it clear, Crista. Gage likes his life just the way it is." Natalie's voice quavered. "The way it used to be, I mean."

Crista shook her head. "Love doesn't just go away, Nat."

Natalie smiled. "Ah. I see what's happening. You and Grant are working things out."

A blush suffused Crista's cheeks. "Well, we're trying. The last few times he flew down—" The doorbell rang, and her eyes lit. "That must be him. He called this morning, said he was canceling his afternoon appointments and coming to see me." She thrust her hands into her hair. "How do I look? I meant to put on some lipstick."

"You look beautiful," Natalie said softly.

It was true. Crista had the glow of a woman about to greet her lover.

The bell rang again. Crista looked towards the foyer, eyes shining.

"I have to go," she whispered. "But I promise, Nat, even if things work out, if I go back to New York, this place will be yours for as long as you want it."

Natalie nodded. "Thank you," she said, and closed her heart against the pain of knowing she would never again race down the hall, as Crista was, to fling herself into the waiting arms of her husband—the husband she loved, and always would.

Gage sat at his desk in his office, frowning over his appointment book.

Was he due in Tahiti this week or next? And St. Thomas. Was that on for the weekend?

He sighed, shoved the book aside, and rubbed his eyes with the heels of his hands. What was that old saying? If this was Tuesday, it must be Hawaii. Or Puerto Rico. Or any place on the planet where there was a palm tree, a stretch of clean sand and an ocean.

He knew where he was right now, anyway. In his office, at the Windsong, in South Beach. He'd flown in last night from…Bali? Yes. From Bali. And the day after tomorrow, he was off again to… It had to be St. Thomas.

"Hell," he muttered, and shoved back his chair.

The flight attendants on the trans-Atlantic and trans-Pacific jets were starting to recognize him on sight.

Hello, Mr. Baron. How are you, Mr. Baron? May I bring you anything, Mr. Baron?

Yes, Gage sometimes wanted to say. A life.

He swiveled his chair around and gazed out the window. The Windsong's guests were splashing and swimming in the pool. Some were lying on lounges, toasting in the sun. They didn't look as if they had lives, but he knew they did. Real lives. Somebody to come home to, at night. Somebody to hold in the dark. To argue with, and laugh with...

Once upon a time, he'd had a life like that.

He'd had Natalie.

She'd been the center of his universe. And he'd been the center of hers. That's what he'd thought, anyway, just as he'd thought their love would last forever. He'd even imagined them growing old together.

Gage swung away from the window.

"You are turning into a maudlin fool, Baron," he muttered.

Those dreams were all in the past. What was the matter with him? Nobody gave any guarantees in life. Besides, his was a life most men would envy. He had power, and money, and status. Women—beautiful ones—hovered around him like bees around honeysuckle.

He had it all.

Gage pushed back his chair and rose to his feet.

Who was he kidding? What he had was a house that rattled with silence and enough Frequent Flyer mileage to start his own airline.

And the emptiness of going to bed each night, knowing that Natalie had left him.

It was time to get past that. It wasn't as if he loved her anymore. Why would he? What was there to love? Once, she had been soft, sweet and warm. Then, before he'd even had time to grasp what was happening, she'd become the antithesis of the girl he'd married. The girl he'd married had given way to a woman who was cold and uncaring of him and the life they'd built together.

She hadn't wanted his baby, either, and that had damn near killed him.

Why?

"Why?" he said to his empty office, with all the plaques and certificates on the walls.

He didn't know the answer. And it didn't matter. He didn't love Natalie anymore. That was all over. It was...

Gage shot out a hand, grabbed the phone and punched in the Palm Beach number, a number he knew by heart and had started to dial a thousand times. It rang once, twice, three times.

Maybe it was a sign that he shouldn't have called. Maybe he ought to hang up...

"Hello?"

He shut his eyes at the sound of Natalie's voice.

"Hello?" she said again, and he swallowed hard.

"Nat?"

"Gage." Natalie reached behind her for a chair and hung on to the back for support. She told herself to speak calmly. "What a—what a surprise."

"Yeah." He cleared his throat. "I, ah, I was just thinking..."

"Yes?"

"I was, ah, I was thinking about you."

Her heart bumped against her ribs. "That's—that's interesting. I was thinking about you, too."

Gage gripped the telephone so hard his knuckles whitened. "Were you?"

She nodded. "Yes," she whispered.

He ran the tip of his tongue over his lips. "What were you thinking? About me, I mean?"

That I don't want to miss you, but I still do.

"Nat? What were you thinking?"

Natalie swallowed dryly. "That, uh, that... That it was a long time since I'd heard anything about our, ah, our situation."

Gage touched his fingers to his temple. For a minute there, he'd thought she was going to say she'd been thinking how she missed him, which only proved what an ass he was. She'd been thinking about the divorce. And that was what he should be thinking about, too.

"Really," he said politely. "Well, that makes two of us. I, ah, I was just looking at my calendar, you know, trying to block out the next few months, and I wondered if you had any idea when our situation might be resolved."

Tears rose in Natalie's eyes. "Jim hasn't mentioned anything definite," she said just as politely.

"No. Well, you know how these lawyers are." Gage laughed pleasantly. "They like to drag things out. Tell you what. I'll check on my end. You do the same on yours."

Natalie thumbed the tears from her lashes. "Fine. We—we don't want this to take any longer than it has to."

Gage shut his eyes. "No," he said gruffly, "we sure as hell don't." The telephone line hummed with silence. "Well, I guess that's all."

"I guess."

"Take care of yourself, Nat."

Natalie bit her lip. "You, too."

Gage waited, the phone in his hand. *Say something, babe. Tell me this has all been a nightmare and I'll be waking up soon...*

But all he heard was the soft click as Natalie hung up the phone.

He sat there for a couple of seconds, his face expressionless. Then, carefully, he placed the telephone back in its cradle, tilted back his chair and steepled his fingers under his chin.

Natalie wanted this over with as soon as possible, did she?

Yeah, well, so did he.

He rose, paced his office from one wall to the other, ran his fingers through his hair until it stood up in little peaks.

Sure, he wanted it over. Not that anybody had ever asked his opinion, sat him down and said, "Well, Baron, how do you feel about the fact that a big, fat hole's about to be put into life?"

Not that it mattered. It was too late for that. The sooner

they ended things, the better. He could go on with his life, she could go on with hers...

Gage's eyes narrowed.

Maybe she'd found another man. The world was ripe with guys like—what was his name? The muscle-bound giant with the pretty face? Hans. Hans, and another zillion like him, all of them eager to hit on a woman as beautiful as Natalie...

On his wife.

Gage roared with fury, snatched up the phone and hurled it at the wall.

Whatever had he been thinking, all these weeks? His wife had said she was leaving him, and except for a couple of pathetic objections, he'd behaved like a doormat.

"Yeah," he growled, "well, we'll see about that."

He grabbed his jacket, flung open the door, and found Rosa standing just outside.

"I thought I heard a crash," she said nervously. "Is everything all right, Mr. Baron?"

"No," he snapped, "but it damn well will be. What day is this?"

"Why...why, it's Thursday."

"Cancel my appointments for the afternoon. And for tomorrow."

"You don't have any appointments tomorrow." Gage strode past her. "Mr. Baron? I said, you have no appointments to cancel tomorrow, sir. You fly to Tahiti in the morning."

"Call Bill Nelson. Tell him he's going in my place."

"But Mr. Baron..."

"Just do it, Rosa."

The door slammed shut, and Gage was gone.

Natalie stood trembling, staring at the telephone while tears coursed down her cheeks.

People always said to be careful what you wished for, and now she knew they were right. She'd wanted a call from Gage and she'd had one. And look where it had left her.

Devastated, that was where. There was no point in denying

the truth anymore. Gage wanted this divorce, and quickly. As far as he was concerned, the sooner she was out of his life, the better.

"Natalie?"

Well, that was fine with her. The more things dragged on, the more confused she got. Why else would she have let herself imagine she still loved him, when she didn't?

She didn't. She didn't...

"Nat?" Crista's voice floated towards her. "I'm home."

Natalie dabbed at her eyes. "I'll be right there."

"Nat, I have such great news..." Crista flew into the room and flung her arms around Natalie. "Grant and I are together again!"

Natalie's heart filled with bittersweet joy. "Oh, that's wonderful!"

"I never expected to make a decision this quickly, but we've talked everything out, and I don't want to be without him another minute. And he surprised me with all these romantic plans. The Concorde, a weekend in Paris... Can you imagine?"

"Umm."

"We're flying back to New York by chartered... Nat? Are you crying?"

"Yes, of course." Natalie smiled through her tears and clasped Crista's hands. "I'm the biggest weeper in the world. Tell me something that makes me happy and I turn into Niagara Falls."

"Aren't you packed yet, darling?" Grant Landon said as he came into the room.

Crista smiled and went into her husband's arms. The look that passed between them was so filled with love that it made Natalie feel like an intruder. She turned away and fought against the burning sensation behind her eyes.

"I'll just go help Addie pack the babies' things..."

To her horror, her voice cracked. Crista looked around, stepped out of Grant's embrace and hurried towards her.

"Natalie! I never meant— Oh, I'm the most selfish person

ever! Here I am, going on and on about how happy I am, and all the while you—''

''And all the while,'' Natalie said with a smile that stretched her lips, ''I'm standing here and wondering, well, what's going to happen to *Designs by Crista?*''

''Nat—''

''Honestly. That's the only thought in my head.'' Natalie gave a laugh that sounded something like a nail drawn across a slate. ''Well, that, and how much I'm going to miss you and the babies and the four-footed guys, but on top of all that I'm wondering, do I still have a job or don't I?''

''Of course you do,'' Grant said. ''Crista's explained how much this business means to the both of you.''

''That's right, Nat. I'll design in New York, but I want you to stay on here and manage the Palm Beach market.''

''The Palm Beach market,'' Natalie said, and bit back another manic laugh. ''I'd love to. And I'll expand, just as you and I discussed. Boca Raton. Maybe Key West.'' She smiled brightly. ''And Miami Beach.''

Crista grasped Natalie's hands. ''Promise me you'll think about what we discussed, okay? About telling Gage the stuff you need to tell him?''

Natalie nodded brightly. ''Sure.''

''I mean it, Nat. You have to—''

The shrieks and squalls of two irritable toddlers suddenly filled the air. Addie stepped into the foyer with the twins in her arms. Annie and Sweetness trailed after her.

''Jennifer tripped,'' Addie said. ''It's her feelings that are hurt, nothing else. And Jessamyn wants her teddy bear, but I can't find it.''

''Here,'' Grant said, ''let me take Jennifer. Come to Daddy, sweetheart.''

''I'll find Jess's teddy,'' Crista said. ''And where's the cat carrier? And Annie's lead?''

''I'll get those,'' Natalie said, because rushing around was better than standing in the eye of the tornado, with time to think about how the world was being pulled right out from under your feet.

Moments later, after hugs, kisses, and, at the very end, some tears, Natalie was alone.

CHAPTER NINE

THE big pink house had never been so silent, or felt so empty.

Natalie stood at the living room window, lost in thought.

A storm was blowing in. The wind-whipped ocean and the oncoming darkness seemed ominous. A flash of lightning lit up the horizon, followed by the dull peal of distant thunder. Wind whistled through the palm fronds and tore at the roof.

Natalie shuddered, pulled the drapes closed and turned on the table lamps. It was as if the weather were trying to match her mood.

There was no way to escape the storm but she certainly wasn't going to indulge in self-pity. There was no reason for it. Crista and the twins were gone, yes, but that was how it should be.

The Landons were together again, and she was happy for them.

"No point in moping," Natalie said briskly...

She slumped back against the wall.

Who was she trying to convince? Her head drooped. She could feel lonely and miserable, if she wanted to. Well, she wanted to.

And it was all Gage's fault.

All these weeks, without a word from him. Then, suddenly, a phone call. A miserable phone call...

She'd been perfectly fine, until then. But after his call, she hadn't been able to get their conversation, or the cool sound of his voice, out of her head.

Crista had sensed that something was wrong.

"Everything all right, Nat?" she'd kept asking as the Landon entourage darted around, packing.

"Fine," Natalie had replied.

And she'd stood in the doorway, smiling and grinning until her lips hurt, waving until the Landon car was out of sight.

Then she'd gone back into the house and things had been going downhill, ever since.

Her footsteps had seemed to echo through the empty rooms, and then the wind had come up and the sky had darkened and, after a while, reality had settled over her like a cloud.

Natalie sighed.

Of course, she was happy for Crista. It was just that it was impossible not to make the comparison between their two lives. Crista had a husband. She had none. Crista had children. She had none. Crista had a home, and a family, and even a dog and cat...

And what did she have?

"A career, selling jewelry," Natalie said into the silence.

And, judging by Gage's phone call, a husband who just couldn't wait to sign his name to a divorce decree.

Natalie frowned. So what? The divorce was what she wanted. It had been her idea, in the first place.

Oh, she was behaving like an idiot.

"An idiot," she mumbled, and she marched to the sofa and started plumping the pillows with far more energy than they deserved.

Her situation was completely different. She'd known that from the beginning. Crista and Grant had been trying to repair a damaged marriage, but her marriage wasn't damaged, it was dead. That was why she'd left Gage. As for being alone, well, what was so awful about that?

Heaven knew she'd spent most of the last few years alone. And, when she had, she'd either drooped around, missing Gage, or simmered with anger over his absence because she'd felt so lonely...but being lonely and being alone weren't the same thing.

Natalie turned on the lights in the kitchen.

Solitude could be wonderful. Hers would be, once she learned to make the most of it. She'd play the music she liked. Do the things she liked. Soak in a tubful of bubbles, if she wanted. Prop a book beside her plate and read through dinner whenever she felt like it...

It sounded like heaven.

"Like heaven," she said brightly...

Her voice broke. She buried her face in her hands.

"What am I going to do?" she whispered.

She still loved her husband.

Natalie flung open the door. Jagged streaks of lightning scarred the distant sky; thunder rumbled over the churning water as she ran down the beach towards the sea.

So what if she loved him? Their marriage hadn't worked, and it was over. That was what she'd wanted. Now, it was what she had.

She had no regrets.

"No regrets," Natalie shouted into the storm, but the wind tossed the words back at her, muffling them in the hiss and roar of the breakers as the sea flung itself angrily against the shore.

"Not a one," she whispered.

The air felt hot and thick, filled with danger and promise. That was how the years ahead would be, too, if she could just get past this terrible despair.

It was exciting, to begin life all over again.

The surf frothed over her toes. Natalie wrapped her arms around herself and looked into the oncoming storm.

She was still young. Perhaps she'd meet another man.

Or maybe Gage would meet another woman.

A lump rose in her throat.

It was possible. More than possible. Hell, it was a certainty. Her husband was handsome and virile. He was successful. Women were drawn to him. She knew that. The bolder ones used to flirt with him right in front of her...not that he'd ever responded.

But he would, once he was free.

Maybe he'd started, already.

They were separated, weren't they? On the very edge of divorce? She'd shoved that fact under his nose every time she'd had the chance. She'd even let him think that maybe there was something going on with Hans even though she knew damn well that Hans had a fiancée back in Amsterdam.

Natalie shivered under the lash of the wind.

Was that why Gage was in such a rush to finish things? Was there another woman, waiting to take her place?

Natalie, the wind sighed, as it swooped around her.

No. Please, no. She wasn't ready to know her husband was in someone else's arms. She never would be, not if she could stand here in the middle of a storm and imagine she heard him call her name...

"Natalie..."

Her heartbeat stumbled. Was that the wind calling her name? Or was it...

Gage's hands, so strong and familiar, fell on her shoulders. He said her name again, turned her towards him, and her heart skipped into overdrive. The sight of him thrilled her. Stunned her. She'd been thinking of him, longing for him, and now he was here, he'd come to claim her, to tell her he loved her and wanted her...

"Dammit," Gage snarled, "what the hell do you think you're doing?"

The smile that begun to tremble on her lips disappeared. Why was he so angry? And what right had he to shake her as if she were a rag doll?

"There's a storm coming in. Do you want to get hit by lightning? Or are you waiting for a wave to carry you out to sea?" His fingers pressed into her shoulders. "You've lost every ounce of sense you ever had!"

Gage knew that Natalie was looking at him as if he'd lost his mind. Well, he didn't blame her. None of this was what he'd intended to say. Hell, he wasn't sure *what* he'd intended to say or do, except confront his wife.

But the sight of her, standing at the edge of the raging surf, had filled him with fear. And then, when she turned and saw him, looked at him as if he were the last man on earth she ever hoped to see...

"Answer, me, dammit." He shook her again, too hard, he knew, but why didn't she say something? Why didn't she say, "Gage, I love you, I need you..."

"And to think—" she said, her breathing fast and shallow,.

"to think I was standing here, wallowing in self-pity because..." She balled her hand into a fist and slammed it into his chest. "You—you arrogant, egotistical—"

"Get up to the house!"

"I do not take orders from you or anyone else, Gage Baron!"

"How about trying some old-fashioned common sense? What in hell's wrong with you, standing out here like this?" His fingers bit into her flesh. "For the last time, dammit, get up to the house!"

Natalie wrenched free. "Who in hell do you think you are?"

Gage looked down into his wife's face, into those eyes that had once blurred with passion at his touch and now burned with angry disdain, and his last bit of control fled.

"I'll tell you who I am," he said roughly. "I'm your husband. And, like the man said, I'm going to be, until death do us part."

He caught her in his arms. She struggled fiercely but he was bigger and far more powerful, and her struggles only intensified what he felt, a primitive fusing of anger and desire as wild as the storm.

"Damn you," Natalie sobbed.

Gage clamped a hand around the back of her head and sought her mouth.

"Damn us both," he said, and kissed her...

And, when he did, she was lost.

This man, her husband, was what she needed. Natalie moaned, wound her arms around his neck and gave herself up to the moment. Gage's rage, his desire, his heat...

She wanted it all.

Her lips parted to the possessive thrust of his tongue. She tangled her fingers in his hair, whispered his name against his kiss. They slipped to their knees in the sand, while the wind howled and the thunder rolled across the heavens.

Gage cupped his wife's face in his hands, slanted his mouth over hers. She tasted of heat and of salt, and of the honeyed sweetness he'd hungered for all these weeks. He slid his hands under her T-shirt and cupped her breasts, and she gasped and lay her hands over his.

"More," she said. "I want more, Gage. I want—"

He pulled back and his eyes met hers.

"What?" he whispered.

"You," she said, "only you."

Her name tore from his throat. He lifted her in his arms, carried her back up the beach to where a cluster of palm trees formed a windbreak, and lowered her to the sand.

Lightning tore the night apart.

"It's been so long," he said against her mouth. "And I've missed you so much, babe. Your taste. Your scent. The feel of your legs, wrapped around me..."

He tried to slow down what was happening but the power of the storm was raging through his blood, and through hers. Natalie arched against him, reached for him, cupped his straining flesh.

"Now," she whispered against his mouth. "Oh, now, please, Gage, my love, please..."

That was what undid him. Not the sweet, drugging taste of her mouth, or the silken heat of her skin, not even the feel of her hand on him. It was that softly whispered endearment he hadn't heard in such a long, long time.

The wind moaned through the trees above them, and Gage gave up the fight.

Natalie's clothing tore apart in his hands. When she was naked, when she lay before him, an ivory offering to the night, he stripped off his own clothing and tossed it aside. She reached for him but he grasped her hands, threaded his fingers with hers, held her arms out to the sides and entered her on one long, velvet thrust, crying out her name as he did. She wrapped her legs around his hips and rose to met him and, as the storm rolled overhead, they were fused in an eruption of white-hot sexual heat.

Natalie stirred beneath him.

"The storm is over," she said softly.

Gage gave her a wicked grin. "Yeah. But it'll be back."

She smiled, too. "I was talking about the thunderstorm."

"Uh-huh. Well, that, too."

Natalie laughed. "I have sand in my hair."

He gave her a sexy grin, rolled to his side, and scooped her against him.

"And everyplace else," he said.

She sighed, snuggled closer, and pressed her lips against his chest. He tasted hot and salty and wonderful.

"What if somebody comes along and sees us?"

"It's a private beach." She could feel him chuckle. "Besides, we'd just tell them we're conducting a scientific experiment."

"Mmm?"

"About electricity. You know, sort of a takeoff on Ben Franklin and his kite."

She laughed again, eased up on her elbow, and kissed his mouth. "An experiment. Of course. Why didn't I think of that?"

"I can see the headline now," he said. "'Violent Electrical Storm Causes Man to Die With a Smile on His Face.'"

"It's too dark for me to tell. Are you?"

"Am I what?" He groaned dramatically. "Dying?"

"Smiling," she said, and gave him a poke.

"That's it. Hit a guy when he's down." Gage stroked her hair back from her face. "Damn right, I'm smiling," he said softly. "Or I would be, if I had the strength."

"Look who's talking. It wasn't me who decided to play in the sand. Honestly, Mr. Baron, do you really think you should be carrying on this way at your age?"

Natalie squealed as Gage grabbed her and rolled her onto her back. "I'll have you know I'm in perfect physical condition, Mrs. Baron." He dipped his head and kissed the tip of her nose. "Besides, I'd never have gotten you back to the house. I mean, you're not the feathery slip of a girl you were when we met…"

"I should hope not. I was fifteen."

"…Or the petite little thing you were when we used to

practice these moves in the back seat of my car on Superstition Butte."

"We did no such thing," Natalie said primly. "We kissed, that was all, even though you used to try to talk me out of my clothes."

"A likely story," Gage said with a wicked chuckle. "I *did* talk you out of them, although I don't recall having to talk very hard. Seems to me you were as intent on finding out what I had in my jeans as I was on finding out what you had in yours."

Natalie sputtered with mock indignation. He grinned and pinned her to the sand.

"But I like you all grown up like this, babe. Curvy. Female. Mature." His free hand drifted lazily down her body, cupped her breast, dipped lower, stroked her belly, then slipped between her thighs. "Oh, yeah," he breathed. "Mature, and sexy as hell."

"Go on. Sweet talk me. See what good it does. You're not going to get anywhere until you apologize for even suggesting I need to lose a few pounds." Natalie bit back a moan as Gage's fingers moved against her. "I am—I am—"

"What?" he whispered.

"I am a sylph." Her words were uneven, her voice increasingly breathless. "And you'd better admit that, mister, if you want—if you expect—" Her lashes fluttered. "I love when you do that."

"This?" he said softly, and moved his hand again.

Natalie locked her arms around her husband's neck. "Yes. Yes, that…"

Gage rolled her beneath him. "Do you, now," he said thickly.

"You know I do."

"But which do you like best? That?" He shifted. "Or this?"

Natalie tunneled her hands into his hair and dragged his mouth down to hers.

"Do I really have to choose?"

"Ah, you're a greedy wench."

"In that case…" She kissed him. Gage slid his hands beneath her, and they spiraled into the darkness again.

The moon was skimming a star-studded sky when they collected the tattered remnants of their clothing and stumbled to the outdoor shower beside the back door.

Gage eyed it warily. "Is it cold water only?"

"I don't know," Natalie replied. "I've never used…" She shrieked as icy water streamed down over them. "You rat," she said, gasping, and dragged him under the spray with her.

Laughing, they let the water wash the sand from their bodies. Then Gage scooped his wife into his arms and carried her into the house, and to bed.

"You just did that because you're afraid I'll beat you up for saying I was fat," Natalie whispered as he lowered her to the mattress.

"Uh-huh," Gage whispered back.

They smiled. Then, wrapped in each other's arms, they tumbled into deep sleep.

Natalie awoke alone, to bright, blazing sunshine…and the numbing realization that what had happened last night hadn't solved anything.

She sat up and pushed her hands through her hair.

There'd been so many questions to ask, so many things to say. Crista had given her good advice. Talk to him, she'd said. Discuss your differences.

But she hadn't. She'd just tumbled into Gage's arms, and into bed, the way she'd done that night at Espada. And what had come of that night?

"Hell," Natalie whispered, resting her forehead on her knees.

Not a damn thing except, perhaps, even more pain because sleeping with Gage had only poured salt on the wound in her heart.

The only thing she knew this morning that she hadn't known last night was that Gage wasn't involved with another woman. Whatever else he was, her husband was an honorable man. If there'd been someone else in his life, he'd never have made love to her.

Color bloomed in Natalie's cheeks.

Wild, incredible love. But then, sex had never been their problem, until she'd lost the baby.

Natalie tossed back the covers and reached for her robe.

Sex had become different then.

She'd yearned for the warmth of Gage's arms. But when she'd turned to him, after she'd healed physically, he hadn't responded.

"I don't want to rush you," he would say when he'd politely put off her advances.

Eventually, she'd realized that what he'd really wanted was to make sure she didn't get pregnant again, that he'd hoped she'd take the initiative and go on the pill or get a diaphragm.

When she didn't, he'd gone back to using condoms, the way he had years ago. Not that it had mattered. After a while, the increasing coolness between them had spilled over into their everyday lives. Sex had turned into something he did and she permitted.

Natalie showered, pulled on a pair of jeans and an oversize blue T-shirt.

Okay. So, somehow or other, maybe because they'd been apart for so long, sex was good again.

Good? She looked into the mirror and picked up her hairbrush. It was great. But you couldn't hold a marriage together with sex. You needed love, and shared dreams. Commitment.

Her hand trembled. Carefully, she put down the brush and curled her fingers over the edge of the dresser.

And wasn't that, really, what having a child was all about? A baby was the embodiment of all those things. A child, created together in an act of love, was a shared, and shining, dream of the future. It was the most perfect way a man and woman had of looking into each other's hearts and saying, yes, we love each other and we always will.

Tears rose in her eyes.

It was so simple. And so complex. It was as old as time,

as new as all the generations yet to come, and if you had to explain it...

How *could* you explain it, when you knew it would be useless?

Life was like a board game. That was the way Gage saw it. Risk this, win that, try something new. Rake in the chips and measure your success by the growing height of the stack. And yes, love your wife, too, in your own way. Shower her with the fruits of your winnings, seek her approval.

And show complete bewilderment when she didn't respond the way you thought she should.

Tell him how you feel, Crista had said. But what could she tell Gage? That there was more to life than winning, more to marriage than passion? He'd shown her how he saw things, time and time again, when he left her alone for days on end while he rushed off to open another resort, when he reached into the nightstand drawer for a condom.

It was why she'd left him, why she couldn't go back to him...

Why last night had been a heartbreaking mistake.

Natalie looked at herself in the mirror.

How simple it would be to blame it on Gage. To say that he'd caught her at a weak moment, that she'd been feeling sorry for herself, feeling alone and abandoned, that otherwise it would never have happened.

But she wouldn't do that. She wasn't going to lie. She'd made a mistake, and she would acknowledge it. She'd go downstairs, confront Gage, tell him that sleeping together had solved nothing, that she still wanted the divorce...

Thud, thud, thud.

What was that? It sounded as if a giant were pounding on the wall.

Thump. Bang. Thump.

No. She looked up. The noises were coming from the ceiling.

The ceiling? Her blood froze. Footsteps. That was what she'd heard. Footsteps, on the roof.

Somebody was on the roof!

How could an intruder have made it up there? Desperately, she tried to visualize the exterior of the house. Was there a drainpipe he could have climbed? A tall ladder? She couldn't even picture a trellis, or a vine. And what about the alarm system?

Oh, hell. What about it? She had never activated it last night.

Thud. Thump. Thud.

Natalie's heart caught the rhythm of the footsteps over her head.

"Help," she said in a tiny voice. "Gage, help."

Stupid, she told herself. Oh, you stupid thing. Gage couldn't hear her, not if she whispered his name so pathetically. Not if he were all the way downstairs... If that's where he was. If he weren't down on the beach, or halfway back to Miami.

If she weren't totally, completely alone.

Her hand shook as she reached for the phone. Okay. She knew what to do. Dial 9-1-1, for the police. Lock her door. Barricade it, if she could manage to shove the heavy dresser across it...

"Oh, damnnnn..."

The shouted curse, and the body hurtling past the window, came at the same moment. The phone fell from her nerveless fingers. Natalie raced to the window, opened it, leaned out—and saw Gage, lying sprawled and unmoving, on the sand.

For one terrible instant, everything spun like a carousel. Then she whirled around, ran from the room and down the stairs. She flew through the house, out the door, to his side.

"Gage?" Her heart banged against her ribs as she dropped to her knees beside him. "Gage, darling, talk to me."

He didn't move. His eyelids didn't flutter. Blood seeped from a jagged cut high on his forehead.

Fear turned her bones to jelly.

"Gage? Oh, please," she whispered, "please, please, please..."

Nothing. Nothing but silence. Had she lost him, this man

she'd always loved, would always love? Surely, life couldn't
be so cruel.

She looked around wildly, searching for help, and saw only
the endless sand and the sea. Natalie shot to her feet, ran into
the house, grabbed the phone and dialed 9-1-1. Her teeth chat-
tered as she gave the operator the address.

"An ambulance," she panted, "I need an ambul—"

Gage moaned. The phone fell from her hand and she flew
out the door and fell to her knees beside him again.

"Darling," she whispered. "Gage, oh, Gage!"

His eyes opened. He blinked hard, focused on her face,
then lifted his hand to her.

"Nat?"

Natalie made a choked sound and grabbed his hand. Tears
spilled from her eyes as she pressed her lips to his knuckles.

"Thank God," she whispered.

"Nat, what happened?"

I almost lost you forever, she thought, that's what happened.

"I was up on the roof. And then—and then..."

"And then you fell," she said, trying to sound stern but
knowing she wasn't succeeding. Gently, she put her hand on
his brow and pushed the hair back from the gash on his forehead. Fear roiled through her again. She took a deep breath
and told herself not to let him see the depth of it. "Lie still.
There's an ambulance on its way."

"Don't need an ambulance. Just help me up, okay?"

"No! You mustn't move, Gage, please don't!"

He shook his head, leaned on one arm and struggled to rise
from the sand. Natalie watched as he struggled, saw his determination, and realized she had no choice. She leaned down,
slipped her arm around his waist and supported him as he sat
up.

"Hell of an entrance," he said, forcing a laugh. The laugh
turned into a hiss and then a groan. "Oh, damn."

"What is it?" Natalie felt the blood drain from her face.
"Gage, I beg you, don't move. You need X rays. A CAT

scan. There's no telling what you've broken. Your legs. Your back—''

''My legs are fine. See?'' He moved one leg, then the other. ''It's my left arm.'' He winced. ''And my head. But that doesn't mean I can't get to the emergency room under my own power. Help me up, babe.''

''No. You can't... What are you doing?''

''I'm—getting—up.''

''You *are* up.''

''No—I'm—not. I—want—to—stand.''

''You can barely talk, let alone... Gage, listen to me! You mustn't...'' Natalie hissed with frustration, slipped her arm around him again and helped ease him to his feet.

''That's better.''

It wasn't. Her medical training began and ended with knowing how to dab antiseptic on a cut but it didn't take a licensed M.D. to know that a man who'd just tumbled off a roof, whose brow was beaded with sweat, who might have a broken arm and did have a gash the size of the Grand Canyon on his forehead, shouldn't be trying to walk.

But Gage was determined to do exactly that. Natalie puffed out her breath and wedged her shoulder under his arm. Together, they hobbled towards the back door.

''You should be lying still,'' she said, ''waiting for the ambulance.''

Where *was* that miserable ambulance, anyway? What was taking so long?

''Just help me to the house. And to my car. And—'' The breath whistled through his teeth as they reached the door. ''Oh, hell,'' he said weakly, and sagged down onto the bottom step.

''''Oh, hell' is right,'' Natalie said with a desperate little laugh, trying to do whatever it took, say whatever it took, to keep him there. ''What on earth were you doing up on that roof, Gage Baron? Did you think you were still twenty-one years old?''

''Twenty-one years...'' Gage flashed a quick smile. ''You remember that summer, huh?''

"Of course I do." Natalie sat down beside him and folded his hand inside both of hers. "We were living in that adorable little apartment, in New York."

"The roach palace, you mean."

"And you took that job working as a roofer, out on Long Island."

"And you worked at the underwear counter at Macy's."

"It was lingerie." Was that the sound of a siren, off in the distance? "I used to tell you that all the time, remember?"

"Yeah." Gage closed his eyes. "I remember everything about that summer, Nat. How you used to kiss me goodbye each morning, as if you might never see me again—"

"I was always afraid you'd fall off one of those roofs."

"But I never did." He opened his eyes, looked at her and managed a quick grin. "Not until today, anyway." His fingers threaded through hers. "I'd almost forgotten that summer, babe. The way you used to take the train out to the Island to meet me every Friday."

"My day off," she said. Yes. Oh, yes, it was a siren. She could hear it clearly now, getting nearer and nearer.

"Uh-huh. You'd pack us a picnic. That cake you used to make, with the chocolate frosting. And sandwiches of that great meat loaf, the one with the ketchup on top. Whatever happened to that meat loaf, Nat? You haven't made it in years."

Meat loaf? she thought. Meat loaf, in that overblown kitchen in Miami Beach? Who'd dare make such a homey thing in such surroundings, much less serve it? Besides, Gage wouldn't have been there to eat it, even if she'd made it.

Tears stung her eyes again, but she shrugged her shoulders. "I don't know. I guess—I guess I just forgot all about it."

"We'd take our picnic out to that stretch of beach we found, the one nobody else ever went to," Gage said, the words starting to slur together. "An' I'd spread a blanket behind a dune an' we'd eat our supper, drink some wine, and then you'd move into my arms…"

"Gage!" Natalie's voice rose. "Gage, don't fall asleep. Stay with me, darling. Please."

"Remember how it was? Making love, with the warm night all around us? With the wind sighing against your skin?" Slowly, his eyes opened. She could see him struggling to focus on her face. "Like last night, here, on the beach. Or all those years ago, back in Texas, when we were kids and I'd drive us up to Superstition Butte." His hand lifted; he threaded it into her hair and cupped the nape of her neck. His fingers were like ice against her flesh. "Where'd we go wrong, babe?" he whispered. "How'd it happen?"

The wail of the siren became a shriek, then stopped. Natalie could hear doors slamming in the driveway at the front of the house.

"Back here," she yelled. "Hurry!"

"Wazzat?" Gage mumbled. "Izzat the amb'lance? Nat, I told you, I don' need…"

His eyes rolled up into his head. Natalie screamed and caught him just as he began to slump over, unconscious.

CHAPTER TEN

THE ambulance attendants said Natalie couldn't ride with Gage.

"You can follow us to the emergency room in your car," the tall one kept saying.

She didn't waste time arguing. Instead, she climbed in behind the stretcher as they loaded Gage into the ambulance.

"Lady," the attendant said, "I told you, you can't do that."

"I've already done it," Natalie said grimly, and sat down on the bench next to Gage's stretcher.

The attendants sighed, looked at the determined expression on her face, then at each other, and shrugged.

"We drive fast, lady," the tall one warned as he slammed the door shut. "Better buckle up and hang on."

Natalie nodded. Then she bent over Gage and brushed her lips against his. "*You* hang on," she whispered as the siren began to wail. "Oh, my love, I beg you. Hang on, tight."

The trip to the hospital seemed to take forever.

Halfway there, Gage moaned and opened his eyes.

"Nat?"

"Shhh." Natalie smiled shakily. "Just lie still. Everything's going to be fine."

"Stupid thing I did, going up on that roof."

"Uh-huh." She took his hand tightly in hers. His eyes began to close. "Stay with me," she said sharply. "Gage? Look at me. Open your eyes."

"Dumb," he muttered. "Real dumb, climbing around up there."

"Talk to me, Gage. Tell me—tell me about the newest Baron resort."

Gage sighed. "...Don' wanna hear..."

"I do! Of course, I do. Is it beautiful? How many rooms does it have?"

"Nat. Sorry. Sorry I fell..."

"Gage." Natalie's voice rose. "Talk to me! Don't pass out on me again!" His eyes shut and tears rolled down Natalie's face. "Please stay with me," she whispered. "Gage, darling..."

"Nat?"

She wiped her nose on her sleeve. "What?"

"I missed you, babe."

His eyelids drooped again, and he was asleep.

Natalie paced the waiting room floor.

She dumped quarters into the coffee machine and forced herself to drink the black sludge that came out of it.

She leafed through a stack of out-of-date magazines, paced some more, drank more sludge, and in between, she marched out to the nursing station and asked if there was any word about her husband.

"He's still in X-ray," they said.

Finally, just when she'd decided it was a lie, that Gage wasn't in X-ray at all, that something terrible had happened and no one wanted to tell her, a nurse appeared in the door to the waiting room.

"Mrs. Baron?"

Natalie sprang to her feet. "Yes?"

"You can see your husband now."

See him. Natalie managed a wobbly smile.

"He's—he's all right, then?"

"He's fine, considering the fall he took. He has a lot of bruises. He sprained the ligaments in his wrist. He has a slight concussion. And he needed some stitches, of course."

"Of course," Natalie said. Her tongue felt thick in her mouth. "But—but he's going to—to live?"

"Oh, my dear." The nurse hurried towards her and put a steadying arm around her shoulders. "Certainly. You mean, you thought...?" She smiled, walked Natalie towards an elevator. "Your husband is in Room 216. The doctor's with him. He'll explain everything."

She heard Gage's voice the instant she stepped from the elevator. He sounded almost like himself—stubborn, determined and demanding to take control.

"I don't see any reason to stay here overnight," he was saying. "And I resent the hell out of having my clothes taken from me. Dammit, Doctor, I am not a ten-year-old."

"No," Natalie said as she stepped into the room. She took a quick look at Gage. A line of neat black stitches ran up his forehead, into his hairline. His wrist was wrapped in what looked like yards of elastic bandage. "No," she said briskly, though her knees went weak, "he's just behaving like one."

"Mrs. Baron." The doctor sighed and took Natalie's outstretched hand. "I'm Doctor Fortas. And, as I've just been telling your husband, we need to keep him overnight, just to be sure his concussion is a mild one."

"I don't have a concussion," Gage grumbled. "All I have is a headache."

"A headache doesn't make a person pass out," Natalie said.

Gage flushed. "I just grayed out, that's all. Anybody would, considering."

"Considering that you fell off a roof, you mean?" Natalie turned to the doctor. "Of course he'll stay overnight. And thank you for your concern."

The doctor nodded. "You can pick him up anytime after I finish my rounds in the morning." He glanced at his watch as he walked to the door. "Say, around nine?"

"Fine," Natalie said.

The door swung shut. Gage glared at Natalie.

"Dammit, Nat! I might have a concussion, but that doesn't mean I'm not capable of making my own decisions."

"Then make an intelligent one. Spend the night here, and I'll come by and pick you up in the morning."

Gage looked at his wife again. Her words had been sharply spoken but there was a softness in her eyes...or was he imagining it? That was what was making him feel so irritable, not the doctor's poking or the nurse's prodding; it was the increasing realization that his accident had come at the worst possible time, just as he and Natalie had come together again.

The memories of last night were real and wonderful, but how about the other stuff he kept remembering, the things that had happened—that he thought had happened—after he'd fallen? Were those memories real, too? Had Natalie kissed him? Had she whispered endearments to him? Had she called him her love, wept over him, or were those all illusions?

Had the blow to his head given him a bunch of false memories, or was there reason to hope—to pray—his wife loved him again?

He needed to ask but how could he, when he was afraid of the answers? If he'd imagined all those things, if they'd been nothing but hallucinations, he didn't want to know it.

Not just yet.

All he wanted to do, at least for a little while, was pretend that the world—their world—was back on track. That was what he'd been thinking when he'd awakened, with his sweet wife asleep in his arms. It was what he'd been thinking when he'd heard a funny sound on the roof, when he'd climbed out and walked around, checking out a patch of cracked tiles the size of China.

He'd still been thinking it when he'd gone sliding down the roof on his butt, like a guy on a suicidal rollercoaster, and as he'd sailed off the edge, his last thought had been that this was a hell of a way to start a weekend, especially the weekend he'd dreamed of, with Natalie back in his life...

"Gage?"

He looked up, and met her gaze.

"Please." Her voice was soft and gentle. "You've had a terrible fall. Spend the night. Let them make sure you're okay. And then tomorrow, I'll take you...home."

Home. Where was that? he wondered. Not in Miami Beach, in that damned empty house.

"Gage? Will you do it?"

He sighed and sank back against the pillows. He'd do anything, when she asked him that way.

"Yeah, okay." He smiled. "Hey, I haven't had a hospital meal since I had my tonsils out. How could I turn down a chance at another?"

Natalie smiled, too. It wasn't easy. It broke her heart, seeing her husband, her big, strong husband, looking so pale and helpless in the hospital bed. She thought of how close she'd come to losing him, of how badly she longed to put her arms around him and tell him that her life would have had no meaning, if he'd died...

But he hadn't. She would never stop being thankful for that gift but, as much as she loved Gage, she knew she couldn't go back to him. His idea of marriage, and hers, were light-years apart. The passion they'd shared would die, as it had before, in the light of cold reality.

Last night had been wonderful, but it was already a memory and nothing more.

Natalie felt a suspicious tingling in her eyes. Don't cry, she told herself fiercely. Whatever you do, don't cry. So she blinked hard, forced a smile to her lips, and clumsily patted Gage's shoulder.

"Good," she said briskly. "That's—that's good. I'll tell the nurse."

He sighed. "The Dragon Lady, you mean."

She smiled again. "I'll tell her you're staying. And I'll— I'll see you in the morning."

In the morning? Gage struggled up against the pillows, gritting his teeth against the pain in his body and the wooziness in his head.

"Natalie? Don't go. Babe, wait..."

But she already had.

The afternoon dragged by.

Gage was grateful when darkness fell, but the night didn't bring him any peace. Every time he dozed off, the Dragon Lady popped in to wake him and ask him if he felt all right.

"I'd feel better if you'd let me get some sleep," he said grumpily.

"We want to make sure you aren't suffering serious concussion," the Dragon Lady said.

He knew that. It was only that staying awake made the
night seem endless, and gave him more time to think about
how quickly Natalie had left, without a kiss, without a
touch—because that pat on the shoulder hadn't been a
touch...

Did she regret the night they'd shared?

Had he imagined the stuff after the accident? The kisses,
the soft words?

By dawn, he was starting to wonder if she'd even show up
to drive him home.

The Dragon Lady threw up her hands when she came in
at eight and found him seated on the edge of the bed, dressed
in his street clothes as well as a man could be dressed when
he only had one hand to work with.

"The doctor will be here soon," she sniffed, and Gage
growled and said he'd damned well better be.

The doctor took one look at him and frowned.

"I take it we're feeling better this morning," he said.

"I don't know how *we* feel," Gage snapped. "I only know
that *I* feel like hell. But I'm not seeing double, I'm not nau-
seous, and I'm not dizzy. So do us both a favor, sign my
release papers and let me out of here."

"Your wife isn't here yet, Mr. Baron."

"She will be," Gage said, even though he didn't really
believe it. But just at that moment the door opened and
Natalie stepped into the room.

"Hi," she said, and his heart swelled at the sight of her.

"Hi. I wasn't sure you'd make it."

Natalie licked her lips. "I said I'd be here, didn't I?" Her
tone was falsely cheerful, as was her smile. "Ready to go?"

"More than ready," Gage said, and he didn't even argue
when the Dragon Lady showed up with a wheelchair.

All he wanted was to get out of the hospital and be alone,
with Natalie—and to work up the courage to ask her about
yesterday, what was real and what wasn't. To tell her that he

loved her and always would, and that she had to come back to him because, God, he didn't want to go on without her.

Most of all—most of all, he wanted to ask her where she was taking him. Home, to Miami Beach? Or home, with her? Because that was where "home" was. Where Natalie was...

"I brought my car. Well, Crista's car."

He nodded. "Good," he said, and cleared his throat. "I'd probably never be able to crawl into the Vette."

He got into the car. She turned on the ignition. Ask her where she's taking you, Gage told himself...

But he didn't.

"How do you feel?" she said as they pulled away from the curb.

Terrible, but he wouldn't tell her that because it would only upset her. That was the way awful little scenes like theirs were played out. He knew that firsthand, courtesy of Natalie's miscarriage. Funny, how they were playing this in reverse. Last time around, he'd been the one driving her home from the hospital. He hadn't taken her there: he'd been in Thailand or Togo or some damned place instead of being at home, with her, when she'd lost their baby...

"I'm fine," he said brightly. "Just fine."

Natalie nodded. He wasn't fine; his face was chalky, his mouth compressed against the pain she knew he must be feeling, but he was going to tough it out. That was so typically masculine...and yet, she knew how sweet and gentle Gage could be. For no good reason, she suddenly thought of the day after her miscarriage, when he'd brought her home from the hospital. He'd insisted on lifting her from the wheelchair into the car, on buckling her seat belt, on giving her the most tender of kisses.

"Are you all right, babe?" he'd kept asking and she, with a hole in her heart that felt as empty as her womb and blaming him—unfairly, she knew—for not having been there when she'd lost the baby...she'd finally told him that she was just fine, dammit, and she'd appreciate it if he'd stop asking.

"Nat?"

She blinked. Gage was looking at her.

"What?"

Where are we going? he thought. "You okay?" he said.

"Me?" She gave a forced laugh. "Of course. I'm not the one who fell off that roof."

"I didn't fall," he said with great dignity. "I slipped."

Natalie raised her eyebrows. "There's a difference?"

"Sure." He flashed a lopsided grin. "If a guy falls, he made a dumb move. If he slips..."

"Yes?"

"Well, he could have tripped over a fallen tree branch. Or stepped on a patch of ice."

"Ice, huh? In Palm Beach, in midsummer?"

"Okay, forget the ice. A pile of wet leaves, maybe. Wet palm leaves."

Natalie smiled. "So, which was it? Wet leaves or a branch?"

Gage laughed, winced, and carefully touched his hand to his head. "Your choice, babe. I'll settle for either one when I have to tell people what happened."

Natalie laughed, too. "In other words, you fell. And here I was, all these years, never thinking I had such a clumsy hus..." Her teasing words faded away. She frowned, cleared her throat, and swung the car towards the curb. "Almost forgot," she said briskly. "The nurse gave me a prescription to fill."

"Nat," Gage said, and reached for her hand, but she was as quick as she'd been last night.

"I'll just be a minute," she said, and slammed the car door shut behind her.

"So," she said in that same brisk tone when she slid behind the wheel again, "you never did tell me what you were doing on that roof."

A muscle knotted in Gage's jaw. She didn't want to talk about anything that really mattered. Well, okay. If that was the way she wanted it, neither did he. One thing for certain. Maybe he didn't know his way around Palm Beach, maybe he didn't recognize these streets, but it was a good bet she was taking him back to Miami. She was making it pretty clear that even carrying on a conversation was more than she wanted.

"A sound woke me, someplace around dawn. Grant had mentioned that the roof leaked, and—"

"You talked to Grant?"

"Yeah. I phoned him a couple of weeks ago."

Natalie looked at him. "You phoned Grant?"

"About the house. Was it okay? Would you be okay, staying in it? That kind of thing. And he said yeah, it was fine. Well, aside from it being about as cheerful as a mausoleum. He said there was an occasional problem with the roof, so when I heard something..."

Natalie nodded in all the right places but she wasn't really paying attention. She'd thought Gage hadn't cared, because he hadn't called her. But he'd called Grant *about* her. In some ways, that meant even more.

Her heart constricted. She didn't want it to but it happened anyway, the same as when she'd first seen him this morning...

"...Figured it might be the sound of tiles shifting on the roof."

Natalie put on her turn signal. "Tiles shifting," she said, and nodded, as if she'd taken in every word.

"Yeah. The storm must have loosened them." Gage's voice turned husky. "You remember that storm, don't you, babe?"

Color flooded her face, but she didn't look at him. "I'll have you home in a little while, Gage. Why don't you put your head back and rest?"

A bitter taste filled his mouth. "Good idea."

He lay his head back and closed his eyes.

Natalie slowed for a stop sign. She glanced at Gage, seated beside her. His eyes were shut. From the even rise and fall of his chest, she thought that he might be asleep.

His color was better today but there was a pinched look around his mouth. He had to be hurting, even if he wouldn't admit it. The nurse had tried to give him some pills before they left but he'd refused.

He'd always been stubborn about stuff like that. Even getting him to take aspirin, if he had a headache, had always been a battle.

He was impossible.

"Impossible," she said softly as she looked over at him again.

Not that she was any better. How else did you describe a woman who took her almost-ex-husband's request that she take him home so literally?

Natalie made a turn onto Ocean Boulevard.

She hadn't even asked Gage if he wanted to stay with her. She'd just made the decision on the spur of the moment, as she stood in the doorway of his hospital room this morning. He'd looked so happy to see her. And she—she'd been so happy to see him.

How could she leave him, when he needed her?

It wasn't as if driving him back to Miami Beach would have constituted some sort of abandonment. She could have telephoned Luz and asked her to move into the house with Gage for a few days, even for a couple of weeks. Luz would have done it, gladly.

Natalie pulled into the driveway that led to the big pink stucco mansion.

And, just in case that hadn't worked, there were other alternatives. Housekeeping agencies. Temporary employment services. Places where she could have arranged to hire an aide, or a nurse.

And wouldn't Gage have loved that? She smiled at the thought. A nurse, marching into his bedroom, waving a thermometer in one hand and a vial of pills in the other.

That would have been worth seeing.

She sighed, shut off the engine, stepped out and went around to the passenger side of the car.

She could have done a lot of things, anything but what she was doing now, but it was too late to have second thoughts.

Besides, this would work out fine.

There was a den on the first floor, with a fold-out sofa, a television set and sliding doors that led onto the patio. It wasn't particularly cheerful but there weren't any cheerful rooms in this house. But she could make Gage comfortable there for a couple of days. When he was feeling better, she'd call Luz and make other arrangements.

Certainly, there'd be no reason to keep him with her longer than that.

She looked at him. What a bad day he'd had. She reached out a hand and gently swept back the dark, silky hair that had fallen over his forehead. The line of stitches stood out in stark contrast to his skin. Ten stitches that would come out in a week.

Well, okay. Maybe she'd let him stay with her until the stitches were out.

But not a moment longer.

Her gaze swept over her husband's face again. There were shadows under his eyes and little lines along the sides of his mouth. And there was stubble on his chin and jaw. Sexy stubble, she'd always called it, when he'd offered to shave on the weekends.

Don't, she'd say, just leave it. Then she'd put her lips to his ear and whisper to him, tell him how that sexy stubble felt, against her breasts, her belly, her thighs.

"Shameless woman," Gage would growl, and then he'd swing her into his arms. "There's only one way to deal with a wanton like you," he'd say, and she'd say, well, she certainly hoped there was more than one way, and he'd flash that wonderfully wicked grin, and then—and then...

Natalie blanked her mind to the memories. Thinking like that would get her nowhere except back into Gage's bed, and that wasn't going to happen again. His injuries guaranteed that, his injuries and her determination. She had faced her moment of truth when she'd awakened yesterday morning.

There was no going back, or denying it.

"Gage?"

"Mmm."

She touched his shoulder. "Gage, wake up."

Slowly, his lashes lifted. "Nat?"

"Yes. We're—we're home. Let me help you into the house."

"Home?" he said, his eyes dark with confusion. He sat up straight, winced at the sudden, sharp pain in his head, and rubbed his hand over his face. "I guess I dozed off."

"Come on. I'll get you inside."

"You drove me...home."

"Of course."

Gage nodded. Home, to Miami. Well, hell, what had he expected? That she'd take him back with her, to that big, ugly house on the ocean? To her sweet-smelling bedroom, her soft bed? That she'd want to hold him in her arms as she'd done the night before last? No way. Natalie had done everything she could to make it clear she regretted that. He'd seen it in her face, heard it in her voice.

"Easy does it," she said, and leaned in the open door of the car. She held out her hand, and he took it. "Put your weight on me."

He nodded, stepped from the car, leaned on her...and looked up, to see the pink stucco, ugly monstrosity of a house looming above them.

Right now, it looked magnificent.

Gage looked down at his wife. Her arm was tucked under his shoulder. Her face—her beloved, beautiful face—was turned up to his.

"You took me home," he said in wonder. "Home, with you."

A flush rose in her cheeks. "Yes. I thought—I figured it would be the best way to—"

Natalie never had the chance to finish the sentence. Gage lowered his head and covered her mouth with his.

CHAPTER ELEVEN

THE kiss might have lasted forever.

Gage was lost in it, and so was Natalie. He drew her into the curve of his arm. She sighed, leaned into his embrace, and a muffled groan escaped his lips.

"Oh!" Natalie sprang back. "Did I hurt you?"

"It's nothing," he said, and bared his teeth in a smile he suspected wouldn't fool anyone. He was right. Natalie was looking at him as if she'd damn near killed him when the truth was that kiss—her kiss—had almost made him feel whole again. It was just that he was starting to feel like one giant bruise, from the top of his head straight down to his toes.

"Here." She wrapped her arm around his waist. "Let me help you up the steps."

Okay, he thought, gritting his teeth against the pain, maybe he wasn't whole again. By the time they reached the front door, he was breathing hard.

Natalie looked worried. "Are you all right?"

"Fine."

It was a lie, and she knew it. His eyes were glassy with pain. Carefully, she led him into the foyer.

"Can you make it just a little bit farther?"

"Sure." He mustered up a smile. "Lead the way."

She steered him down a hall. His head felt as if it might explode at every step, which wasn't such a bad idea. Then, at least, the little man drilling through his skull would go away.

The room she led him to was big enough to host a small convention—if the convention were held in Transylvania. The walls were dark mahogany, the ceiling was paneled, and the furniture was covered in cracked oxblood-red leather, with enough decorative tacks to start a small hardware store. Moth-eaten animal heads stared down glassily as Natalie eased him onto an enormous sofa.

"Cheerful," he said.

Natalie smiled. "The first week or so, I kept waiting for Count Dracula to appear."

She spoiled the atmosphere by first opening the damask draperies that covered the windows, then the blinds. Sunlight, and the sound of the sea, came pouring in. Gage tried not to wince, but he couldn't quite manage to pull it off.

"Too bright?"

He nodded. "Just a little."

"Sorry." She closed the drapes, angled the blinds. "Is that better?"

Darkness would have been better, but then he'd have had to admit he ached all over. Natalie would want him to take the pills she'd bought, and they'd probably put him to sleep. And sleep was the last thing he wanted, just now.

What he wanted was his wife, back in his arms.

"Uh, yeah. Yeah, that's fine."

"Good. I'll just go get you a blanket and a pillow."

"Nat—"

"You stay put, Gage. You know what the doctor said."

He looked at her blankly. "No. What?"

"You're to take it easy. Stay off your feet."

"When did you talk to the doctor?"

"I didn't." She smiled. "But doctors always say that."

God, her smile was wonderful. So wonderful, that he managed a smile in return.

"Only in bad movies. Trust me, Nat." He sat forward and began to rise from the sofa. "I'm perfectly..."

Oh, hell. The world went gray, and he sank back against the cushions just in time. Natalie rushed to his side.

"Put your head down," she commanded.

He knew better than to argue. Besides, her cool hand was already on the nape of his neck, soothing away the pain. She knelt beside the sofa, her fingers still soft on his skin.

"Better?"

He looked up, into her beautiful eyes. "Yes. Thanks."

"Well, it was my duty." She smiled. " I couldn't let you pass out, could I? If real men don't whine, they sure as heck don't faint."

Gage's brows knotted. "How'd you know that?"

Natalie's smile tilted. "You told me, a long time ago."

"Did I?"

"Uh-huh." She rose to her feet. "Way back in the days when you and I still had things to talk about."

There was no heat in the words. Still, they rocked him. "What do you mean? We've always had—"

"I'll get those linens," she said, and swept from the room.

After a moment, he lay back on the sofa. What kind of crack was that? They'd always had things to talk about. What they'd lacked was the time to talk, but that wasn't his fault. Natalie had her clubs and her charities, he had a business to run.

Gage yawned. He was tired. So tired.

He tumbled into deep, dark sleep.

When he awoke, the room was filled with the soft, gold haze of midafternoon sun—and, to his surprise, he felt better.

Carefully, ever so carefully, he put his good hand on the sofa cushion and eased himself up.

"Hell," he whispered.

"What's the matter?"

The sound of Natalie's voice startled him. He jerked around and saw her rising from the depths of a wing chair near the fireplace.

"Gage? Do you hurt?"

"No," he said. It was almost the truth; the maniac playing the kettle drums in his head had reached a crescendo, but now he was backing off.

"Liar," Natalie said gently.

She handed him a glass half filled with water, then held out her hand. He looked at the capsules that lay in her palm and then he sighed, took one of them, and swallowed it. She took the glass from him, reached past him and set it on the table. He caught a whiff of her perfume. She smelled of wildflowers. He'd always loved that scent. She'd worn it for years, ever since…

"I bought you that," he said, "didn't I?"

"What?"

"That perfume." He sniffed. "It smells great."

"Yes. Yes, you did." She knelt down beside him, the way she had before he'd fallen asleep, but this time she lay her hand against his forehead. "Are you okay?"

"Mmm." He put his hand over hers. "That feels terrific." Natalie tried to pull her hand free but his fingers tightened on hers. "No, just leave your hand there for a minute. It's nice and cool."

"I—I can get you an ice pack…"

"I'd forgotten all about that," he said softly. "The perfume. It was the first present I ever gave you. You were seventeen—"

"Sixteen."

"Uh-huh." His eyes met hers. "We drove out to the lake…"

"We drove up to Superstition Butte." Natalie tugged her hand loose. "Lift your head a little, so I can fluff your pillow."

He lifted up. She leaned towards him. Her hair brushed lightly against his cheek.

"You're right. It was Superstition Butte. You were wearing that white dress, the one with the little pink flowers."

"They were blue flowers," she said softly. "And after we'd parked, you dug into your pocket and took out a beautiful little package, all wrapped in silver paper."

"Yeah." Gage chuckled. "You'll never know how my knees knocked together when I walked up to that perfume counter at Walgreen's." His eyes met hers, and his smile dipped. "That was the night I touched your breasts, for the very first time. Do you remember that, babe?"

Did she remember? How could she not? That first hesitant brush of his fingers against the softness of her flesh. The rasp of his shadowy beard against her nipples. The heat of his breath, of his mouth.

"Yes," she said softly, "I remember. That's where—it's where everything began for us. At Superstition Butte."

"We'd been up there before. But we'd always stayed in the car." Gage's voice roughened. "That night, I took that old blanket out of the trunk. We got out, and I spread the blanket over that little patch of grass."

Natalie swallowed. "You should be resting, Gage. I mean, you just got out of the hospital…"

"You opened the perfume." His voice was soft. He reached out and ran the back of his hand over her cheek. "You put some behind your ears."

"Gage," she whispered, "please…"

"And then I took the bottle from you, babe, and I put some of the perfume on my finger and I drew my hand down, along your throat, to this little hollow, right here."

Natalie's eyes drifted shut. She began to tremble. "Don't. Oh, don't…"

She said the words because it was right to say them, but they had no conviction. She wanted this: the stroke of his calloused fingertips against the softness of her skin, the whisper of his lips down the length of her throat as he nuzzled open her blouse.

His hand brushed the swell of her breasts, and she moaned.

"Natalie," he whispered. "My sweet. My love."

"No." Natalie pulled away. She stood up and shook her head. "We can't."

Desire knotted in his belly and hoarseness his voice. "We can. You're my wife."

"Not anymore," she said, and she swung away and ran from the room.

He must have dozed off again.

When he awoke, the room was dark except for a single lamp throwing out a soft light in the far corner.

Gage sat up, took a deep breath and struggled to his feet. Then he hobbled down the hall, until he found the bathroom.

"Whoa," he said softly when he saw himself in the mirror. He not only felt like a giant bruise, he looked like one.

Two black eyes. Stitches. The elastic bandage. At least the pain in his head and wrist had given way to a generalized, all-over ache.

He flushed the toilet, washed his hands, splashed cold water on his face. Then, moving slowly and carefully, he made his way towards a bright light at the far end of the hallway.

Natalie was in the kitchen, seated on a high stool before the sink, slicing carrots into a pot. Sometime during the afternoon, she'd changed into white shorts and a white T-shirt. Her feet were bare; her toes curled gracefully over the rung of the stool.

She looked beautiful, and, as always, incredibly sexy.

But sexy wasn't what he felt.

What he felt was a love so strong, so powerful, that, just for an instant, it was difficult to breathe.

This woman was his wife. Once, she had been the center of his life. And then, somehow, he had almost lost her. He'd thought she'd stopped loving him, but she hadn't. He was certain of that. It was just that she was afraid of giving in to that love, and he didn't know why.

But he was going to find out.

Fate had put them together again. For a day, a week…whatever the time granted him, he had to use it to win Natalie back. And, once he did, he'd never let her slip away from him again.

"Hi," he said.

Natalie swung towards him. A flush rose in her cheeks, and he wondered if it was because she'd been thinking about him.

"Hi, yourself. I thought you were asleep."

"I was." He hobbled into the room and leaned back against the sink. "Seems as if I've slept the day away."

"Well, you didn't get much sleep last night. Each time I phoned, the nurse said…" She stopped in midsentence. Then she turned away, picked up a wooden spoon and stirred the pot. "I'm just making supper. I can bring you a tray and serve you in the den, if you like."

"You checked up on me," he said softly.

"Hmm?"

"You called and asked the Dragon Lady how I was doing."

"Yes. I called, a couple of times." A dozen times. Two dozen. Once every half an hour, until finally the nurse had told her she was being a nuisance. "I, ah, I didn't want to get to the hospital and find out they weren't ready to release you."

"The Dragon Lady should have told me." A smile curved his mouth. "It might have improved my disposition. I thought you didn't give a damn."

Natalie spun towards him. "I always gave a damn," she said fiercely. "You were the one who didn't, the one who—who—" She glared at him. Then she tossed aside the spoon, reached for an oven mitt and opened the oven door.

"The one who what?" he said, bewildered.

"Forget it. Just—just sit down, and we'll have supper."

Gage nodded. Something was happening here and he didn't know what it was, only that it was dangerous. And, God, the last thing he wanted to do tonight was start a quarrel.

He kicked out a chair, sat down, and searched for a safe topic.

"So, uh, so, what's doing with the Landons?"

"They went to Paris."

"They worked things out, then?"

"Yes."

"Great. They're nice people."

Natalie slammed the oven door. "Yes, they are."

"It's a hell of a thing, when two people who love each other lose their way," he said cautiously.

Natalie opened a drawer and took out a handful of silverware. "I agree."

"Sometimes—sometimes, it just happens."

She looked up. "Nothing 'just happens,'" she said softly.

"No. No, I guess not." Gage cleared his throat. "So, how did they get together again?"

"Grant and Crista?" Natalie shrugged. "I don't know, exactly. I guess they discussed the things that were keeping them apart."

"What things?"

"Things. You know, just—things."

Natalie put the silverware on the table. Gage picked it up and arranged it on the placemats.

"What if two people don't really know what things are keeping them apart? What then? I mean, what if the guy hasn't got a clue?"

Natalie's back stiffened. "That's a real problem. The very fact that he doesn't have a clue says—it says a lot about what's happened to their relationship."

"Well, why doesn't the woman just tell him?"

"Maybe she's tried to. Maybe he just hasn't listened. Maybe things have gone too far."

"So, what is the guy supposed to do? Is he supposed to ask, 'What happened? Why did things go wrong?'"

There was a silence. When Natalie spoke, her voice was soft and shaky. "Sometimes—sometimes, it's too late for that. The what and the why don't matter. They both can just tell that—that it's over."

Gage reached out and caught hold of her hand. "It isn't over," he said fervently. "Not for me. I never stopped loving you, babe. Never, not for a minute." His fingers curled around her wrist. "Did you stop loving me?"

His heart thumped like a gypsy's castanets while he waited for her answer, for what he'd see in her eyes. At last, she turned and looked at him. Her eyes were glassy with unshed tears but he couldn't tell if the tears were for him, for herself, or for what had become of them.

"Nat? Did you stop loving me?"

She knew this was the moment. All she had to do was look him in the eye and say yes, she had stopped loving him. Their marriage would really be over. Gage would never touch her again, never come after her. She would be free of him, of his love...

"Babe?"

Natalie raised her head. Their eyes met.

"No," she said brokenly. "Never. I always loved you, Gage. And I always—"

She got no further. His chair tumbled over backwards as he rose, took her into his arms, and crushed her mouth beneath his.

"I love you," he said, his lips a breath from hers. "Nat, sweetheart, I love you so much."

And she loved him. What was the use in pretending? She loved him, she'd always loved him, ever since she was sixteen. She could make a life without him—she knew that, now. But, oh, she didn't want to. She didn't want to.

Her arms wound around his neck. Her head tilted back, and her lips parted to the thrust of his tongue. Sanity, logic, reason...all of it fled in the sweetness of Gage's kiss. This, *this*, was all that mattered. Being in his arms. Tasting his kisses. Knowing his love.

His hand slipped up, under her shirt. She gasped at the feel of his fingers on her back, on her belly, oh, on her breasts.

"Your wrist," she whispered, but he shook his head and kissed her again and again, until she felt as if she were whirling in space.

"Take this off," he growled, and she helped him strip away her T-shirt, her shorts, her bra.

"And you," she whispered, her fingers trembling as she opened the zipper on his jeans.

Gage moaned her name, threaded his fingers into her hair and bent her back over his arm. He lowered his head; his lips closed on her nipple and she sighed with pleasure.

"Now," he said as she reached for him. "Now, babe, right here, because I can't wait, I can't."

"Don't wait," she whispered, and arched against him. "Please, Gage. I want you inside me..."

His body stiffened at the sound of her words. He caught his breath, buried his face in her hair.

"Gage?" Natalie framed his face with her hands and lifted it until they were looking into each other's eyes. "What is it? Have I hurt your wrist? Your head? Oh, I knew we shouldn't have done this, I knew—"

He lifted his hand, lay a finger gently over her mouth to

silence her. Everything had to be perfect tonight. He knew it, knew he would lose her, otherwise.

"You haven't hurt me," he said softly.

"Then, what is it?"

"I don't have anything with me, Nat."

Her forehead creased in puzzlement. "I don't understand."

"I don't have a condom, babe. I didn't use one the other night, either." He saw her expression begin to change and he took a deep breath. "I'm sorry, sweetheart. We'll have to wait. God knows, we don't want to get you pregnant..."

He saw the blur of her hand, felt the sharpness of her palm as it connected with his face.

"No," she said bitterly. "God knows, we sure as hell don't."

"Babe," he said, but it was too late. She was gone, and he was alone.

He paced the den. The glassy-eyed animal heads stared at him dumbly and he thought how good it would be if they could speak to him, but they remained mute. Finally, when he couldn't stand their silence anymore, he flung open the patio door and strode down the sand to the sea, but the waves and the moonlight had no answers, either.

And, damn, he needed answers.

Either he was crazy or Natalie was. And he was tired of trying to figure out which.

After a while, he walked back to the house. The light was on in one of the rooms upstairs. Let her sit upstairs and sulk. Or brood. Let her do whatever it was she was doing, because he didn't care. Forget about needing answers. Hell, he didn't even know the questions.

No way.

Not anymore.

There was a decanter of something or other on a sideboard in the den. Gage took a glass from one of the shelves above it, opened the decanter and poured. He raised the glass to his nose and sniffed.

"Gawd," he said, shuddered, and tossed half the stuff down.

He dropped into the corner of the leather sofa, picked up a magazine and opened it. The words danced on the page but he kept staring at them in grim determination to take his mind off Natalie. It didn't work; he was still trying to think about the magazine article and not her when she came marching into the room. As soon as he saw her, he knew he'd been waiting for her, listening for the sound of her footsteps.

"I'm sorry I hit you," she said. He could almost see the icicles hanging from the words as they left her mouth. "Considering your condition, I mean."

"What condition?" Gage stretched his lips in a tight smile. "I'm fit as a fiddle. And anyway, I probably deserved getting slugged." He reached for his half-empty glass and raised it towards her in mock salute. "Not that I know what the hell I got slugged for."

"No," she said, even more coldly, "you wouldn't."

"And I don't suppose you'd care to explain it to me?"

"I didn't come here to discuss what happened. I just thought you might like to know what you missed for supper."

Gage yawned.

"Meat loaf," she said.

He looked up. Her hands were balled on her hips; her eyes were steely.

"And chocolate cake." Her smile was feline. "For dessert."

"Meat loaf?" he said after a minute. "And chocolate cake?"

"That's right." She looked down and brushed an imaginary speck of lint from her shorts. " I also thought you'd like to know that I just tossed it all into the garbage."

And, with that, she turned on her heel and marched away.

Gage sat there for a while, trying to piece things together, but only somebody who was into reading minds could have managed that. Finally he got to his feet and made his way to the kitchen. Natalie was there, scrubbing furiously at a pan.

"Look," he said, taking the first step as cautiously as a

tightrope walker above a bottomless chasm, "I'm trying to figure out what's going on here. But I'm not getting anywhere, Nat. I really don't understand any of this."

She looked up at him. "I know you don't. That's the worst part."

"Natalie. Natalie, sweetheart…"

Natalie hurled the pan against the wall. "Don't you sweetheart me," she cried. Then she burst into tears and ran from the room.

And Gage…Gage was finally ready to admit the rope was too thin and the chasm too wide.

He needed help.

He took the phone into the den, shut the door and sat down in a chair. The stares of all those moth-eaten animal heads seemed focused on him as he punched in a number.

Travis answered on the first ring.

"Trav? It's Gage."

"Gage? What's the matter, man? You sound—"

"Listen, I, ah, I just wanted to ask you a question."

"Yeah? Gage, you sure you're okay? You sound—"

"I'm trying to talk quietly, dammit! I don't want Natalie to hear."

"Oh." Travis cleared his throat. "What's up?"

"Well…" Gage cleared his throat, too. "Listen, when one person wants a divorce but the other person doesn't…"

"Damn. Is that still on? I kept hoping you and Nat would—"

"The person who doesn't want it can fight it, right?"

"Well, I guess, but why would I have wanted to? I sure as hell didn't love—"

"I'm not talking about you. I'm asking you for legal advice. What can a man do, when his wife says she loves him but then does everything she can to prove she doesn't love him, after all." Gage shut his eyes. "I know I sound crazy, Trav, and I'm sorry. It's just that this is confusing."

"Love, you mean." Travis gave a funny laugh. "Yeah, it sure is."

"Trav, look, I know you don't understand. I mean, I know you're not in love, that you've never really been in love..."

"Love sucks, man." Travis's voice roughened. "A man loses his equilibrium, turns into some jackass he doesn't recognize. And for what? All so a woman can drive him crazy, turn him into a—a gibbering idiot."

"Trav? Are you okay?"

"Yeah," Travis said, and gave that funny laugh again. "I'm fine."

"You sure? You don't sound okay."

"Listen, Gage, I'm—I'm kind of in the middle of something here. You want to know if you can stop Natalie from going through with this divorce? The answer is no, pal. I'm sorry to tell you this but if she wants out, she's out."

Gage nodded. "Yeah. I kind of figured..." He blew out a breath. "Thanks anyway."

"Gage? Don't let her go. Don't ever let the woman you love go, not if you have to turn cartwheels to keep her."

"Dammit," Gage said, "I *have* been turning cartwheels..." But he was already talking to a dial tone.

He sat there for a couple of minutes, trying to figure out what to do next, when, suddenly, the phone rang.

"Hello?" he said cautiously.

"Gage?"

Gage frowned. "Slade? Slade, how in hell—"

"Travis called me."

"Travis? But I didn't give him this phone number."

"Welcome to the age of the chip," Slade said dryly. "His Caller ID box gave it to him, buddy. You didn't have to. Where are you, by the way? I don't recognize the area code."

"I'm in Palm Beach. And don't ask, okay? It's a long story."

"Yeah, well, I just phoned to tell you that Trav is right."

"He is? About what?"

"About not letting Natalie get away from you."

Gage sighed. "For a couple of freewheeling bachelors, you guys sure are full of advice for the lovelorn."

"I'm not joking, Gage." Slade's voice dropped low. "You

love a woman, you're a damn fool if you ever let her walk
out of your life. You understand?''

Gage's brows rose. ''Not really. I mean, I agree with the
advice, but aren't you the guy who's watched legions of
broads march into the sunset?''

Slade made a sound that wasn't quite a laugh. ''Legions
don't count for a damn, bro. It's just one woman, *the* woman,
who does. A man finds her, he should have his head examined
if he lets her get away. You got that?''

Gage nodded. ''I've got it. But you're the last one I'd expect—''

''Tell me about it,'' Slade said, and the phone went dead.

Gage stared blindly at the wall. His brothers made it sound
so easy. Hell, it *had* been easy, back when he and Natalie
had first met.

When they'd first met.

''Yes,'' he murmured, and put the phone to his ear again.

Half an hour later, he scaled the stairs. That was how it
felt, anyway, by the time he reached the open door to
Natalie's room.

She was at the window, gazing out across the sea. When
he said her name, she spun around and stared at him.

''Gage? How did you—''

''Natalie,'' he said in a voice that left no room for questions, ''change into jeans. Grab a jacket. And meet me downstairs.''

''What for?''

''We're taking a trip.''

''Are you out of your mind?''

''No,'' he said as he headed out the door. ''Yes. Hell,
maybe I am.'' He turned and looked straight into her eyes.
''Remember what you said tonight? About where we began?''

Natalie's forehead creased. ''I have no idea what you're
talking ab... You mean, what I said about Superstition
Butte?''

Gage nodded. ''That's right, babe. And that's exactly
where we're going. Back to where it all started. To
Superstition Butte.''

CHAPTER TWELVE

IT SEEMED a strange time for Gage to be making bad jokes.

"Superstition Butte," Natalie said, and laughed.

Gage didn't laugh. He didn't even smile.

"That's right. And…" He checked his watch. "And we've only got a few minutes to get ready, so you'd better hurry."

Natalie stared at him. Her smile began to fade when she saw his grim expression and realized he was serious.

"Are you crazy? We are not going to Superstition Butte. We're not going anywhere. It's the middle of the night…"

"Ten minutes, Natalie." He spoke calmly, resolutely, and she began to worry. Maybe his mild concussion hadn't been mild at all. Maybe he'd really suffered some kind of brain injury.

What came next? Hallucinations? Coma?

Maybe he was going crazy.

If so, he was certainly doing it in a strange way. He'd made a decision. They were going to Espada, and that was that. When she tried to point out that he was a mass of bruises and stitches, that his wrist was wrapped in enough elastic bandage to last an ice hockey team a month, he looked at her as if *she* were crazy to think of letting minor things like those get in the way.

So Natalie tried a different approach.

"Gage," she said in the sort of reasonable tone she thought best to use with someone who'd lost his grip on reality, "you might be in the mood to go to Espada, but I'm not. Really, you can't just expect me to—"

"Yeah, babe," he said, and gave her a steely look, "I do expect it. Now, are you going to get out of those shorts and into a pair of jeans by yourself, or am I going to do it for you?"

She gave a strangled laugh and started to tell him that

169

somebody who looked like a leftover from a Mad Max movie was hardly a threat...but then she changed her mind. Gage was battered but not beaten. The look in his eye said it all. He'd follow through on his promise, all right, even if it meant another visit to the emergency room.

So, to keep him calm, she put on jeans, grabbed a jacket, and followed him downstairs.

"I'll drive," she said, trying to sound as if nothing out of the ordinary were happening.

Gage took her arm. "No need."

He opened the front door and she saw the taxi in front of the house.

"Get in," he said calmly, and he got in beside her and told the driver to take them to the airport.

Half an hour later, seated beside him in the passenger section of a small, sleek chartered jet, Natalie was wondering which one of them had lost touch with reality, Gage for making these arrangements or she, for letting him carry them through.

"Are we really going to Espada?" she asked as the plane raced down the runway.

Gage looked at her. "I said we were."

"It's the middle of the night!"

"It's nine o'clock." His lips twitched. "Seems to me we've stayed up later than this, once or twice."

"But why? Why go to Espada?" Natalie struggled to keep her voice from rising. "When you're hurt? When nobody's expecting us? What's the point?"

"One," he said, ticking the answers off on his fingers, "we're not really going to Espada. We're going to the Butte. Two, as long as I'm not flying this thing, my being hurt isn't a problem. In fact, I'm looking forward to catching a couple of hours sleep. Three, Abel's expecting us—"

"Abel? You phoned Abel?"

"I did. He's meeting us with a car. And four, if you don't mind, I think I'll go back to item two and get some shut-eye."

"But," Natalie sputtered, "but—but—"

It was useless. Gage had already tipped back his seat, closed his eyes, and drifted off.

After a while, she tipped back her seat, too, and tried to do the same thing. It was impossible. She was too upset, too confused, too everything.

She looked out the window. The sky was bright with stars. The moon was an ivory globe. Back at the beach, the water would be as warm and silken as the air.

It was the kind of night to spend in the arms of a lover. In Gage's arms.

But she'd never go into his arms again.

Natalie's throat constricted. She loved him. She always would. Even after his callousness tonight, even though he didn't understand her—she loved him. That would never change. There was no use pretending that it would.

And she knew that Gage loved her, loved her very much—in his own way.

The trouble was that loving each other wasn't enough.

They saw life differently. They wanted different things from it. That was what had driven them apart, and that was what would keep them from ever living together again.

Natalie closed her eyes.

It hadn't always been like this. When they'd married, the only thing they'd wanted was to be together. To build a life, and share it.

When had it all changed?

She could remember how proud of him she'd been, when Gage started Baron Resorts, and how happy she'd been to be part of the empire he was building. She'd learned to organize a dinner for twenty on half an hour's notice, to always have an overnight case ready so that she could fly halfway around the world with him minutes after he phoned. And yes, she'd loved the wonderful things he'd given her. She'd felt like a princess, living inside a fairy tale. And when she'd discovered she was pregnant, her happiness had only grown.

Tears stung her eyes.

But the fairy tale hadn't had a happy ending. She'd lost her baby. Then she'd lost her husband.

This weekend, just for a little while, she'd thought—she'd let herself think—that things could work out. She loved Gage, she'd told herself. And he loved her. That was enough. People who loved each other didn't just turn and walk away from a marriage.

Oh, but they did. Walking away was the only way to save whatever remained of self-respect, the only way to keep love from turning into something dark and ugly.

Walking away was exactly what she had to do.

I don't have a condom. Gage's voice rang inside her head. *God knows, we don't want to get you pregnant.*

Tears seeped from under her lashes.

Those words had marked the end of everything. She knew if she stayed with Gage, she'd hear them every time he reached for her. She'd think of the child they'd lost, the child he'd never wanted. And, eventually, whatever respect and love she had for her husband would die.

It was far, far better to live with the memory of love than to watch it die.

Natalie dragged the back of her hand across her eyes but it didn't help. The tears spilled hot and fast down her cheeks.

Compromise, Crista had said, but compromise wasn't possible, not for Gage and her. You couldn't compromise on a dream.

She turned her face towards the window, towards the welcome darkness of the night.

Oh, what a glorious dream it had been. So bright, so shining...

Gradually, her tears slowed. And, at last, she fell into a deep, troubled sleep.

Gage woke as the plane was starting its descent.

Natalie was curled in her seat beside him, her face turned to the window, her breathing deep and even.

"Natalie," he said softly. She didn't stir. "Babe?" He leaned closer. Her scent rose to him, a heady mix of the perfume he loved and her soft, silky woman-heat. He longed to rub his chin against her hair, to take her in his arms and wake her with kisses, but instinct told him now wasn't the time.

There were things to talk about first, questions to ask, questions to answer.

"Nat. Wake up. We're landing."

Natalie murmured something in her sleep. She turned to him, burrowing against him the way she used to, her head against his shoulder, her hand on his chest, and all his resolve fled. He tipped her face up and gently brushed her lips with his.

"Gage," she sighed. The hand that lay against his chest moved up and curled around his neck. The soft caress swept through him like fire. He groaned, drew her closer, and kissed her more deeply. Her mouth softened under his. Her lips clung, then parted...

And she awoke.

For an instant, as her eyes opened, he saw love and desire shining in their depths. But then she pushed free of his embrace and sat up stiffly, behaving as if they were strangers, her eyes cool, her expression distant.

"Sorry," she said. "I—I must have been dreaming."

Of me? Gage almost said, but he didn't. He was afraid of her answer. Maybe he was kidding himself. What possible chance did he have of winning Natalie back, if she could turn to stone in his arms as he kissed her?

But she hadn't been stone, not when they'd made love the other night, not even a few hours ago in the kitchen.

The plane touched down. Gage unbuckled his seat belt. Natalie loved him. She'd already admitted it. He had to keep reminding himself of that.

And he had to find a way to make her tell him why loving just wasn't enough.

It was hot outside the plane, the air so thick and humid it seemed to cling to their skin.

"I'd forgotten what it can be like here in midsummer," Natalie said as they stepped into the Texas night.

"It'll be cooler up on Superstition Butte."

A breeze plucked at a lock of her hair, and she thumbed it behind her ear.

"Is that really where we're going?"

Gage looked at her, his eyes dark and unsmiling. "I've never lied to you before, babe, and I'm not going to start now. I said Superstition Butte and that's exactly where we're going."

Abel was waiting alongside the runway, leaning against a battered pickup truck. One of the hired hands stood alongside.

"Mr. Gage, Ms. Natalie," Abel said. His brows rose as Gage stepped into the glare of the headlights. "My, oh, my," he said, "don't you look interestin'? You taken to ridin' Brahma bulls?"

Gage grinned. "Riding a Brahma would be an improvement. You brought the car?"

Abel jerked his head towards the hired hand. "Bob drove her. She's parked right over there."

Gage shook hands with the two men. Then he took Natalie's elbow and walked her into the darkness. After a few yards, she came to an abrupt stop.

"I don't believe it!" She swung towards Gage. He could see the smile on her face. "That can't be what I think it is...can it?"

"If you think it's my old heap from high school," he said, smiling back at her, "it's exactly what you think it is."

She stared at the beat-up old Chevy. "But I thought you'd junked it, years ago."

"I never had the heart. I took the tires off and parked her in the old barn, asked Abel to turn the engine over from time to time. I called him tonight and he put her back together, ready to go." Gage opened the door. "Come on, babe. Get in."

Natalie hesitated. There were so many memories in that car, all of them sweet with the promise of youth and hope...

"What are you worried about, Nat?" Gage flashed a grin. "I figure she'll hold out for the trip to Superstition Butte and back."

Natalie looked at the old Chevy. The car probably would hold out. But would she?

"Nat?"

She looked at her husband. His smile was soft with promise, the way it had always been when he'd come by to take her out, more than a decade ago.

"Wanna go for a ride?"

His husky voice sent a rush of anticipation through her blood. The invitation was the same, too, and the implied promise.

She knew she ought to say no, tell him that what she wanted was to get on the plane and go straight back to Palm Beach...but suddenly there was something magical in the night, something magical happening right here, and only a fool would have done anything to spoil it.

It was almost as if the old car knew the way to the butte all by itself.

The road was the same as it had been, years before. It was a one-lane dirt track that cut through the heart of Espada, then wound into the hills to end high atop a red-rock butte with only the stars and the moon for company.

When they reached it, Gage shut off the ignition.

Silence, broken only by the sigh of the night breeze and the soft hooting of an owl, settled over the car.

Gage took a deep breath and turned to Natalie. "Remember what we said this afternoon? About the Landons, and how sad it was when two people who love each other lose their way?"

She nodded and looked down into her lap, at her tightly folded hands. Her hair swung over her cheek, hiding her face.

"Yes. But sometimes.... Sometimes, it's a lot more complicated than that."

Gage reached out and touched his hand to Natalie's cheek, gently pushing back her hair so he could see her.

"Yeah. You're right. And I don't understand how that happens, babe. I mean, just look at us. When we started out, it was all so simple."

Natalie sighed. "I know."

"A boy, a girl…" He smiled, leaned back in the seat and looked up at the moon. "Do you remember coming up here?"

"Of course."

"Damn, but it's a miracle we didn't turn this old car into a heap of smoldering ashes." He chuckled, reached for her hand and laced his fingers through hers. "All those nights…"

"Gage, I don't think it helps to talk about—"

"And even that one afternoon." He looked at her. "You remember that afternoon, babe?"

Did she remember? Natalie felt the color rise in her cheeks. "I—I remember."

"We must have been crazy, drivin' up here, makin' love out there, on that old blanket, with the sun beatin' down…"

She didn't want to smile, but she had to. "Don't look now, cowboy, but your drawl's back."

"What drawl?" Gage said. "Why, darlin', ah doan have no drawl. None A-tall." He smiled at her, his heart soaring when she smiled back, and then he cleared his throat. "I didn't really bring you here to talk about old times."

Natalie caught her lip between her teeth. "I didn't think you had. It seems an awfully long way to go, just to play 'remember when,' especially when we—when we won't want to remember all this in just another few—"

Gage stopped the terrible flow of words with the gentle brush of his fingers across her mouth.

"Don't say it." His voice was gruff with emotion. "Not until you've heard me out."

"Gage." Natalie's voice quavered. She took a breath and began again. "Gage, talking won't change anything."

"Answer just one question, Nat." He shifted in the seat, cupped the nape of her neck with his hand and looked into her eyes. "Will you do that for me?"

She hesitated, then nodded. "All right. One question."

Gage's gaze seemed to bore into the depths of her heart.

"A couple of hours ago, I asked you if you still loved me. And you said you did. Is that true?"

Natalie swallowed hard. "Yes. I—I'm willing to admit, I still—I still feel something for—"

He kissed her. Lightly, gently, his mouth as soft as silk on hers.

"And I love you," he whispered.

Natalie's eyes filled with tears. "I know. But love isn't—"

Gage kissed her again. And, despite everything she'd told herself, she couldn't keep from responding to the kiss.

She drew back, lifted her hand, touched it to his face, then dropped it back into her lap.

"Love—love isn't always enough," she said, her voice trembling.

"Love is everything," he said harshly. "Love is all there is. All the rest doesn't mean a hill of beans."

"That's not true. Not even love can keep a dream alive, Gage."

"What dream? Dammit, the only dream I ever had was you."

"At first. But then—then you wanted other things. And I don't blame you," she said quickly. "A man needs to—to leave his mark on the world, and Baron Resorts is your mark, one you can be proud of."

"Is that what you think Baron Resorts is, Nat? A monument to my ego?"

"No. I didn't mean—"

"I built Barons for us." Gage's mouth twisted. "For you and me. Yeah, I'm proud of what I've done but I thought you were proud of it, too."

"I was. I am—"

"Are you telling me wanting to succeed was wrong? That I shouldn't have gotten pleasure out of being able to give you the kind of life you deserve?"

"I'd have been happy if—if the life you gave me meant living in that apartment in Manhattan."

Gage snorted. "The roach palace?"

"*Our* palace. Our home."

"Oh, right. Some home that was. The rug we bought second-hand. The furniture we picked up at that yard sale in Brooklyn..."

"It wasn't perfect."

"The understatement of the year," Gage said.

"At least we chose those things ourselves, instead of letting some—some tender-toes decorator do it for us."

Gage blinked. "Tender-toes?"

Natalie flushed. "Maybe you like all that stuff. The tiny chairs nobody can sit in. The leather couches so big people slide off them when they sit down. All those miserable mirrors, the ones that let you see that last night's mousse is already sitting on your hips—"

"Are you serious?"

"Of course, I'm serious."

"You don't like our house?"

Natalie sighed. "It's not the house, it's the things in it. I know I'm hurting your feelings, but—"

Gage laughed. "Oh, babe, if you only knew how I despise all that stuff." He took a lock of her hair between his fingers and let the softness of it slip against his skin. "Maybe not the mirrors," he said with a little smile. "It's kind of nice, getting to see my beautiful wife in triplicate as she steps out of the shower."

Natalie blushed. "I hate those mirrors," she said firmly.

"Okay. The mirrors go. What else?"

"Gage, this is pointless. Refurnishing the house won't—"

"You like the kitchen, don't you?" He sounded almost desperate. "All those—what do you call them? Those state-of-the-art appliances?"

"All those appliances Luz uses more than I do."

"Hey." Gage's brows drew together. "You're not going to tell me you didn't want Luz, either, are you?"

"Luz is wonderful." Natalie lifted her chin in defiance. "But you seem to think I prefer going to silly charity luncheons to making a meat loaf. Well, I don't. Didn't. I mean, it isn't important anymore, now that we're—now that we're getting divorced, but I really liked to take care of our home, Gage. I didn't need Luz to do everything for me."

Gage blew out his breath. "Let me get this straight. You're telling me you hate our house. You don't like Luz doing things instead of you. You think those luncheons are silly. And you're not exactly ecstatic about the life I've given you."

"No. I never said—"

"That's right. You never said, not one damned word." His mouth thinned. "What else have you been hiding from me, Natalie?"

"Me?"

"Yeah, you. Because there are only two things *I* haven't told *you.* One is that I always hated the way that jerk decorated our home. The other is that I don't *ever* want to lose you. Not ever." Gage cleared his throat. "So the only secrets left are yours, Natalie."

"I don't have any secrets—"

"You damn well do. At least one, babe. The one that's making you leave me, even though you love me."

Natalie bowed her head. "It's too late," she whispered.

"The hell it is!" Gage caught her chin in his hand and forced her to look at him. "Tell me what's hurting you and we'll work it through."

"We can't." Her voice broke. "We can't work it through, because it's something we don't know how to talk about it. We both know what it is—"

"I don't know, dammit!"

"You do! Oh, it doesn't matter. No amount of talking could help us, Gage, because this is about my dream, not yours. It's the reason my heart is breaking, the reason we can't make our marriage work…"

She twisted away from him, opened the door and flung herself from the car. Gage cursed, threw open his door and went after her.

"It sure as hell is worth talking," he roared when he caught her and spun her towards him, "because I'm lost here, Natalie. What's this dream? What is it that you want that I haven't given you?"

"Your child!" The words tore from her throat and flew

into the hot silence of the night. "Your baby, Gage—yours, and mine."

Gage stared at his wife in disbelief as she buried her face in her hands, her sobs racking her body as if they came not from her throat but from the very depths of her soul.

"A child?" he said. "Our child?" He stared at her. "But...but...but..."

He clamped his lips together in frustration. Was that all he could say? He was not a man who was ever at a loss for words but, right now, he could find none.

Natalie wanted his child? She'd left him, because she wanted his child? Because he hadn't given her the one thing she wanted, the one thing *he* wanted?

He wanted to shake her. To yell at her, for not telling him. To hurl invectives at the sky, because of the months and years of stupid, painful misunderstanding...but most of all, he wanted to take his wife in his arms and kiss her. Tell her that her dream was his dream, that his heart was almost bursting with happiness.

He reached for her, then pulled back his hand. Whatever he said now would be far more important than anything he'd ever said to her in all the years they'd been together. He knew that, just as surely as he suddenly knew that they were not at the end of their marriage but at the beginning.

"Nat," he said softly, "you're wrong. Sweetheart, you're wrong. We *can* talk about it. We *must* talk about it."

Natalie lifted her head. Tears were streaming down her face and her nose was running. He pulled out his handkerchief and handed it to her, and thought that she had never looked more beautiful.

"Don't say anything you'll regret," she said hoarsely. "Don't make any promises for my sake. It's why I never spoke about—about the baby we lost, Gage, because I knew that if I—if I let you know how badly I ached for him, how desperately I wanted to become pregnant again, you might give in and say, okay, we'll have a child, if that's what you want, the same way you—you went along with my pregnancy that first time."

"What?" he said. "What?" Anger roughened his voice. He caught hold of her, forgetting about his sprained wrist, and a sharp pain shot up to his shoulder but he didn't care. Enough was enough. "I went along with your pregnancy? Is that what you think?"

"Yes. And I know it wasn't easy. It meant a change in the way we lived, that I wouldn't be able to travel with you—"

"Dammit, Natalie! Where did you ever get such a crazy idea? I walked on air for days after we found out we were having a baby."

Natalie blinked. "You did?"

"Hell, I was so excited, I drove everybody nuts. 'I'm having a baby,' I'd say in the middle of a board meeting." Just for a second, a grin tilted across his mouth. "And they'd all look at me as if I'd gone crazy until finally Johnny Miller cracked, 'Did you tell your wife?'"

"But—but you never said..."

"I didn't think I had to."

"Actually—actually, I thought you were happy about the baby. I didn't realize the truth until—until after I lost it."

The remembered guilt of that day rocketed through him.

"I wasn't there. I know, babe. And I've been trying to make peace with it ever since. I should have been home. I didn't want to be away from you but I figured it was best to get the traveling done before..." He swallowed. "Before our baby came."

Natalie stared at him. "You did?"

"I didn't want to be the kind of father Jonas had been. I wanted to be there for my kid, you know, go to school plays, to ball games, read him bedtime stories. I know it was crazy but I had this idea in my head that I could get everything out of the way so I could be there from the minute our child came into the world, until... Nat? Sweetheart, don't cry."

"Oh, Gage..."

"It damn near killed me," he said gruffly, "when I realized you didn't want to try again."

"I did. Oh, I did. I thought you were the one who didn't." Natalie smiled through her tears. "The first time you used a condom, I cried my heart out after we'd made love. I told myself it would be all right, that I could live without having your child. And maybe I could have—but you and I kept growing further and further apart. You traveled more and more..."

"Because it killed me, to see how you kept me at a distance, when I was home."

"I thought you wanted that kind of life. And—and I began to hate you for wanting it instead of a family."

Gage bent his head and kissed her mouth. "I love you," he said huskily. "I always have. I always will. Do you understand that, sweetheart?"

Natalie laughed, and her tears glistened like starlight in her eyes. "Yes," she said, "oh, yes."

They kissed again, and then Gage tucked Natalie's head against his shoulder.

"You remember the things we used to do up here?"

She drew back and looked up at him. "Picnic, you mean?" Laughter danced in her eyes.

"Yeah. Picnic. And—other stuff."

"Not really," she said solemnly. "I think you're going to have to remind me."

Gage kissed her again. Natalie made a soft little noise in her throat, one that had always made his pulse beat quicken. His tongue slipped into her mouth and she wound her arms around his neck.

"Umm. I think I'm beginning to remember..."

He nuzzled her hair from around her throat and nipped gently at the tender spot behind her ear.

"Good," he whispered. "Let's see if we can stir your memory a little more."

He looked deep into her eyes. Then, slowly, he undid the buttons on her blouse, fumbling a little because of his injured wrist. The blouse fell from her shoulders. The rest of her clothing followed until, at last, she was naked.

Gage looked at his wife, his beautiful wife, and felt the sudden tightness in his throat.

"Natalie. Sweetheart, I've missed you so terribly."

"Touch me," she whispered. "Gage, please. Touch..."

Her breath caught as he cupped her breast and bent to it. He drew the beaded tip into his mouth, then kissed his way down her body and dropped to his knees before her. Natalie's head fell back as his mouth sought and found her, and she cried out her pleasure to the stars.

Gage stood up and kissed her, so that she tasted their mingled passion on her lips.

"Undress me," he said softly.

Natalie did. She unbuttoned his shirt, smoothing her palms over his hard, muscled chest. She opened his belt, the fastener at the top of his fly...and hesitated.

"Are you sure you're up to this?" she said in a breathless whisper, and he laughed softly, caught her hand, and brought it to the powerful swell of his arousal.

"You tell me, sweetheart."

When, together, they'd stripped away his clothes, he took her hand, kissed the palm, and led her to the old Chevy.

"Unless I miss my guess, babe, our old blanket's still in the trunk. But you'll have to help me. It'll take more than one hand to make us a bed in the grass."

When the blanket lay spread out in the moonlight, Natalie looked at her husband and smiled.

"Gage Baron," she said solemnly, "you're going to get us in a whole lot of trouble."

The words were the ones she'd whispered to him so many years before. And, as he had that night, he kissed her and drew her down with him to their improvised bed.

"I'll stop if you want me to," he whispered just as he had all those years ago.

Natalie lay back, her arms around his neck. "Never," she said fiercely. "Never stop, Gage, because I love you. I love you. I—"

He kissed her hungrily, ran his hand over the body he knew and worshiped. And then he drew back.

"Babe?"

"Yes?"

"Wouldn't it be wonderful if we're lucky enough to make our baby tonight, right here on Superstition Butte?"

Natalie laughed with happiness. "Yes." She reached up and framed the beloved face of her husband in her hands. "Oh, yes, darling, that would be—"

Gage entered her on one long, sweet, possessive thrust. She sobbed his name, lifted herself to him, and gave herself up to love.

The wind sighed through the trees. The moon slid from the sky. The owl flew home on silent wings.

And just at the moment Natalie cried out in Gage's arms, a shooting star flamed like a fire-tipped arrow across the black Texas sky.

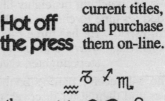

Coming Next Month

HARLEQUIN PRESENTS®

THE BEST HAS JUST GOTTEN BETTER!

#2031 WEDDED BLISS Penny Jordan & Carole Mortimer
Two complete stories in one book to celebrate Harlequin's
50th anniversary.

THEY'RE WED AGAIN! Penny Jordan
Belle Crawford found herself seated next to her ex-husband
Luc at a wedding. They'd been divorced for seven years so
everyone expected fireworks—and there were...fireworks
sparked by passion!

THE MAN SHE'LL MARRY Carole Mortimer
Merry Baker had been cruelly jilted by the father of her child
eighteen years ago, so she'd never really considered men or
marriage. But after meeting handsome Zack Kingston she had
to change her mind....

#2032 HER GUILTY SECRET Anne Mather
Alex's life had fallen apart when his wife died, and he'd lost
custody of his baby daughter. Now he was suspicious of his
gorgeous new employee, Kate Hughes. Was she involved with
his fight to get his daughter back?

#2033 THE PRICE OF A BRIDE Michelle Reid
Mia agreed to marry millionaire Alexander Doumas so that
both he and her father would gain from the deal. But how
could Mia's real reason for marrying Alex be kept a secret
when she shared such passion with him every night?

#2034 ACCIDENTAL BABY Kim Lawrence
To Jo, gorgeous Liam Rafferty was simply her best friend.
Until one night they accidentally got too close—and Jo
found herself pregnant! Unexpectedly, Liam insisted on
marriage....

#2035 THE GROOM'S REVENGE Kate Walker
India had been about to say "I do" when Aidan, the fiancé
she loved and desired, accused her of being a gold digger
and promptly jilted her. Now Aidan was back wanting
revenge: he'd help India's family, but for a price—India....

#2036 SLEEPING WITH THE BOSS Cathy Williams
Victor Temple worked with his assistant Alice, all day, every
day. Their relationship had always been strictly business—
until now. Suddenly Victor had seen behind her neat
professional disguise and found the real, passionate Alice....